Also by
THE BEASTLY BOYS

Werewolf versus Dragon

Bang Goes a Troll

The Jungle Vampire

Battle of the Zombies

SEA MONSTERS
AND OTHER DELICACIES

BY THE BEASTLY BOYS
ILLUSTRATED BY JONNY DUDDLE

SIMON AND SCHUSTER

First published in Great Britain in 2008
by Simon and Schuster UK Ltd,
A CBS COMPANY
This paperback edition published in 2010.

www.beastlybusiness.com

The right of Matthew Morgan, David Sinden and
Guy Macdonald to be identified as the authors of this work have
been asserted by them in accordance with sections 77 and 78
of the Copyright, Design and Patents Act, 1988.

Simon & Schuster UK Ltd
1st Floor, 222 Gray's Inn Road, London WC1X 8HB

A CIP catalogue record for this book
is available from the British Library.

ISBN: 978-1-84738-838-4

1 3 5 7 9 10 8 6 4 2

Printed in the UK by CPI Cox & Wyman, Reading, Berkshire RG1 8EX

www.simonandschuster.co.uk

TONIGHT,
LOOK UP AT THE MOON.
LOOK AT IT CLOSELY.
STARE AT IT.
NOW ASK YOURSELF:
AM I FEELING
BRAVE?

CHAPTER ONE

It was night and, under the cover of darkness, a fishing boat motored across the sea. In the boat's wheelhouse, a tall man in a long fur coat was clutching the wheel, steering through the choppy waves. He glanced across the water towards the black silhouette of an old oil rig. It stood heavy in the sea like an iron giant.

The man smiled, then cut the boat's engine. He poked his head from the wheelhouse. 'This is the place,' he said. His face looked twisted like a rotten apple core. 'Hurry up, Blud! Hurry up, Bone! It's time for a spot of fishing. Get me a sea monster! Now!'

On the deck of the boat, a big man with

1

greasy hair and a thick black beard dipped his hand into a wooden crate. He took out a hand grenade and pulled out its pin with his teeth. He threw the grenade into the sea, then leant over the side of the boat, listening. From deep underwater came a muffled boom as the grenade exploded. The boat shuddered. 'That'll give it a headache,' he said. 'Come on, you big beast! Up you come.'

At the rear of the boat, a small man in a ragged suit looked up from a bucket. His face was pale green and his chin was wet with sick. 'Did we have to come here?' he groaned. 'I don't like the sea.'

The boat was rocking from side to side in the waves.

The man in the fur coat stepped across the deck and gave the small man a kick. 'Stop whingeing, Blud, you pathetic whelk.'

'Yes, Baron Marackai. Sorry, Baron Marackai,' the small man, Blud, replied, scrambling to his feet. He wiped the sick from his chin with a soggy red rag.

The man in the fur coat, Baron Marackai, pulled a torch from his pocket. He switched it on and shone it out to sea. 'There must be one here somewhere,' he said.

Blud and Bone gazed across the water, following the beam of light.

Baron Marackai looked at them. 'Well, don't just stand there,' he told them. 'Throw in more grenades! Blast the beast out of the water!'

'Yes, Baron,' both men said, running to the crate. 'Whatever you say, Baron.'

Blud and Bone each took out a handful of grenades. They pulled the pins out and threw the grenades overboard. 'Bombs away!' they yelled.

From deep beneath the waves came a succession of muffled explosions. Blasts belched from the depths and the boat lurched. Blud and Bone clung to its side. They threw more grenades, and the sea erupted in plumes of water. Flapping fish showered on to the deck.

Baron Marackai paced up and down, shining his torch over the dark water.

'Excuse me for asking, Sir, but what do you want a sea monster for?' Blud asked.

Baron Marackai licked his twisted lips, then turned to face the small man. 'So that we can eat it,' he said.

Blud grinned. Bone rubbed his big fat belly.

'We'll boil it alive then scoop out its brains and chop off its tentacles,' Baron Marackai told them. 'It's the most delicious beast imaginable.'

'But what if we get caught, Sir?' Blud asked. The small man's eyes flicked left and then right, looking out to the dark sea, checking there were no other boats in sight.

'Those fools won't stop me this time,' Baron Marackai said. He rubbed the small stump of flesh where his little finger was missing then held up his right hand. 'Now repeat after me. Death to the RSPCB!'

Blud and Bone held up their right hands and folded down their little fingers. 'Death to the RSBPC,' they said.

'The RSPCB, you numbskulls!'

Blud and Bone sniggered.

Baron Marackai stamped his snakeskin boot. 'Enough!' he said. 'Now get to work! I have a plan that will send the RSPCB to their doom.'

'That's what he told us last time,' Blud whispered to Bone.

Baron Marackai picked up a dead fish from the deck of the boat and slapped it across Blud's face. 'Don't talk about last time!' he spat. 'Just get me a sea monster! And leave the RSPCB to me.'

Blud and Bone threw grenade after grenade, hurling them into the sea. Explosion after explosion echoed beneath them. The sea erupted. Fish and seaweed showered down, and the boat heaved and rolled.

Baron Marackai shone his torch over the side, sweeping it back and forth lighting the waves.

A huge tentacle broke the surface of the water. 'There!' he called gleefully. 'Sea monster to starboard!'

The tentacle rose upwards, twirling high in the air. Then it crashed down, smashing against the boat. The Baron clung to the side as Blud and Bone slid across the deck, slamming into the wheelhouse.

'Get up, you idiots!' the Baron shouted.

Blud and Bone scrambled to the side of the boat and peered over the edge. Beneath the waves they could make out the dark shape of a huge beast with giant tentacles.

'It's enormous!' Blud said.

'It's gigantic!' Bone said.

'What did you expect, you nincompoops? It's a sea monster!'

As the huge beast scraped the hull of the boat, the Baron ran inside the wheelhouse.

Blud and Bone cowered as tentacles reached up, coiling over the deck. The tentacles were long and thick and covered in barnacles. They wrapped around the stern and smashed the hauling winch from its fittings.

The boat was tilting in the water.

'It's angry, Sir,' Blud called, crawling for cover behind the wooden crate.

A tentacle whipped towards him, grabbing

7

him by the leg and dragging him across the deck. 'Help!'

Bone picked up a large iron anchor and started whacking the tentacle with it.

Baron Marackai poked his head from the wheelhouse.

'DON'T LOSE IT, YOU IMBECILES!'

BEASTLY
BUSINESS

CHAPTER TWO

Ulf woke up feeling the sun hot on his face. He crawled from the straw, rubbing his eyes, and stepped out through the door of his den. The sun was high in the sky above Farraway Hall and, on the rooftop, he could see Druce the gargoyle creeping over the tiles peering down the chimney pots.

Ulf got on to his quad bike and kick-started its engine. He rode up the path along the side of the paddock, stopping at the edge of the yard. He hopped off and went into the feed store to grab a sausage.

'Up late last night, were you?' he heard.

Ulf turned, looking out through the feed

store's large wooden doors. Flying towards him from the flower garden was Tiana the fairy. She sparkled as she flew. 'Everyone's been up for hours,' she said. 'I've been collecting nectar.'

In her hand was a basket made from a hazelnut shell. It was full with yellow syrup.

Ulf opened the cold-meats fridge and took out a sausage. 'I overslept,' he told her.

All night Ulf had been awake watching the moon. It was nearly full and there were just two days until his transformation.

He gobbled the sausage then wiped his hairy hand on his T-shirt. To look at him, Ulf could easily be mistaken for a human boy. But every month, on the night of the full moon, he would undergo a complete physical change, turning from boy to wolf. Ulf was a werewolf.

'Do you want to help me collect nectar?' Tiana asked.

Ulf shook his head. 'I promised I'd give Orson a hand with the trolls. Besides which, nectar's for fairies.'

He licked the sausage fat from his lips and stepped out of the feed store into the yard.

'Suit yourself,' Tiana said. 'More for me!' She flew back to the flower garden in a trail of sparkles.

Ulf hopped on to his quad bike and rode through the yard, past the fire zone, the hatching bay and the quarantine unit. 'Open,' he called. A voice-activated gate opened in front of him. He stood up on his foot bars and rode out into the beast park.

Farraway Hall was the headquarters of the RSPCB, The Royal Society for the Prevention of Cruelty to Beasts. It had been Ulf's home for over ten years, ever since he'd arrived as an orphaned werecub. It was a rescue centre for rare and endangered beasts.

Ulf bumped along the track past the aviary, a high-netted enclosure containing the winged beasts. He glanced through the wire mesh and saw three griffins tearing at a lump of meat. Next door to them, a mantabird was hovering like a flying carpet.

Ulf accelerated to the biodomes where the extreme-weather beasts were housed. As he passed the desert dome he saw a fountain of sand shoot up from the blowhole of a sandwhale. In the snow dome a yeti was beating its chest, and in the storm dome he could see electrodactyls diving into the eye of a hurricane. Ulf glanced back as a conductor lizard flicked out its tongue, catching a bolt of lightning.

He sped away, looking up to Troll Crag, a rocky hill dotted with caves. Halfway up, he could see Orson. Orson was a giant. He was walking towards the mouth of a cave, holding a tree trunk in each hand.

Ulf rode up the rocky hill to meet him.

'Afternoon, Ulf,' Orson said, laying the tree trunks on the ground. The giant dusted his hands on his shirt. They were as big as shovels.

'Sorry I'm late,' Ulf said, jumping off his quad bike. 'I overslept.'

'Can you help me clear this cave, please?' Orson asked. 'The trolls have been banging about and the roof's fallen in.'

Orson ducked his head inside the cave, and Ulf followed.

The cave was large and smelt of troll dung. A pile of rocks and boulders lay on the ground. At the back, Ulf could see chewed bones where the trolls had been eating, and huge footprints leading down two dark tunnels. From deep underground, he could hear the faint echoing sounds of trolls snorting and grunting.

As Orson began clearing the larger boulders, Ulf helped him, shifting the smaller rocks and stacking them outside the cave.

It was hard work, and a smelly way to spend an afternoon, but Ulf liked being with Orson. While they worked, the giant told Ulf stories about what it was like in the wild.

Ulf longed to see the wild. All afternoon he tried to imagine what it must feel like to live there, as he carried rock after rock, stacking them outside the cave.

When the cave was clear he rested in the sun, looking out from the top of Troll Crag. From high up he could see over the whole of the beast park, over the Dark Forest to the Great Grazing Grounds. To the South, Dr Fielding's Jeep was parked on the dockside by the seawater lagoon.

'What's Dr Fielding doing?' he asked.

'A sea beast's coming in,' Orson told him, stepping out of the cave. 'She's getting everything ready.'

Ulf could see Dr Fielding heading to the marine store by the examination bay. Dr Fielding was the RSPCB vet. She mended the sick and injured beasts that were brought in from the wild.

'What kind of sea beast?' Ulf asked.

'A sea monster,' Orson told him. 'A boat's bringing it in. Dr Fielding got the phone call this morning.'

In the distance, out to sea, Ulf could see a fishing boat heading towards the lagoon. 'Can we go and help?' he asked.

Orson picked up the two tree trunks lying on the ground. 'Let's get these in, then we can,' he said.

The giant smashed the tree trunks over his knee, snapping them in half. He carried them into the cave and Ulf helped him wedge them upright so they stood like pillars supporting the roof.

'That should hold it,' Orson said.

He stepped out, brushing the dust from his bald head, then strode off down Troll Crag. 'Come on, Ulf,' he called.

Ulf jumped on to his quad bike and bumped down the rocky slope, following Orson round the edge of the marsh and Sunset Mountain, then along the shore of the seawater lagoon.

Dr Fielding was standing on the dockside. She turned and smiled as Ulf and Orson came towards her.

'Just in time,' she told them. 'Orson, could you guide the boat in, please?'

'No problem,' Orson said. He strode off along the dockside to the automatic sea gates at the mouth of the lagoon.

'Ulf, would you give me a hand with the examination bay, please?' Dr Fielding asked.

16

Ulf jumped off his quad bike and followed Dr Fielding to a concrete rectangular enclosure full of water. It was set into the dockside and sealed off from the lagoon by an underwater gate. This was where sea beasts were examined.

'Can you open it up, please?' Dr Fielding asked him.

With both hands, Ulf twisted a metal wheel on the dockside. At the front of the enclosure an underwater gate slowly opened.

As he looked up, he saw the fishing boat motoring across the lagoon. Its front was tilting upwards, and from its stern, steel cables were pulling something heavy through the water.

Dr Fielding waved from the dockside. 'Over here, Captain Crab,' she called.

The boat motored slowly towards the examination bay and an old fisherman poked his head from the wheelhouse. 'Ahoy there,' he called. He had a curly white beard and was wearing a blue fisherman's cap. 'Captain Crab at your service, Dr Fielding. One sick sea monster needing urgent attention. Found it floating in the marine reserve, out by the old oil rig.'

'Can you bring it into the examination bay, please?' Dr Fielding called. 'We'll need to take a proper look.'

Captain Crab looked at the huge dockside enclosure. 'Blimey!' he said. 'This place has changed a bit since old Farraway's day.'

He ducked his head back into the wheelhouse. The boat pulled into the examination bay. Ulf heard a clang and then a grating sound as the steel cables slackened at the back of the boat, releasing the sea monster in the water.

Ulf looked down. Beneath the boat, bundled in a net, he could just make out an enormous beast with thick coiling tentacles.

'You can reverse out now, Captain,' Dr Fielding called. 'Ulf, can you close the gate, please?'

The boat's engine belched black smoke as

Captain Crab reversed out of the examination bay. Ulf turned the wheel on the dockside, and the underwater gate clanged shut.

The sea monster was secure.

Orson came striding along the dockside, rolling up his shirtsleeves. He reached into the water to pull the net from the beast.

'Not with your hands, Orson!' Dr Fielding told him. 'It's venomous! Use a grappling hook.'

The giant pulled back his arm. From the marine store, he fetched a long pole with a hook on its end. He pushed it into the water and heaved the net from the sea monster.

Ulf stared in amazement as the sea monster's huge tentacles uncurled, writhing and thrashing, churning the water. They reached to the edges of the examination bay.

'Orson, would you mind showing the Captain where to moor his boat?' Dr Fielding asked.

She opened a hatch in the dockside and began climbing down a ladder to the underwater viewing gallery. 'Come on, Ulf,' she called. '**Come and have a look at this sea monster.**'

CHAPTER THREE

Ulf climbed down the long metal ladder, following Dr Fielding to the bottom of an underground room deep beneath the dockside. One wall of the room was made entirely of glass. This was the viewing window for observing sea beasts. It looked out underwater into the examination bay. Through it, Ulf could see the sea monster.

'It's gigantic,' he said.

'It's a Redback, one of the rarest sea monsters on the planet,' Dr Fielding told him. 'An adult female, about one-hundred-and-fifty years old.'

The sea monster resembled a huge armoured octopus, covered in a hard spiky shell of red

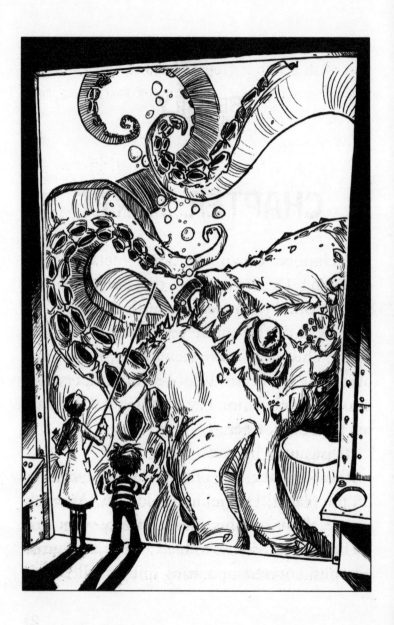

coral and barnacles. It had a craggy-looking face with bulging green eyes, and eight massive tentacles, each as thick and as long as a tree trunk.

'What happened to it?' Ulf asked.

'Captain Crab found it floating in the Farraway Reserve. It's not normal for a sea monster to come to the surface. They're bottom dwellers.'

The sea monster appeared to be struggling to swim. Three of its tentacles were hanging limply while the other five were reaching for the sides of the examination bay, trying to grip the walls. Its massive body was rolling and turning. A tentacle whipped out and crashed against the viewing window. Ulf could see oily black suckers pulsating on the glass.

'What's wrong with it?' he asked.

'I'm not sure exactly,' Dr Fielding replied.

She was walking up and down the viewing gallery studying the sea monster's movements.

'Look here,' she said, reaching with a cane across the window, pointing in turn to each of the sea monster's tentacles. 'Its left distal tentacles appear to be paralysed, and its ventral and medial tentacles are displaying involuntary spasms.'

Suddenly, the sea monster's shell began trembling. It let out a loud rumbling bellow that shook the window of the viewing gallery.

Ulf stepped back from the glass.

'It's in pain,' Dr Fielding said.

'Can you mend it?' Ulf asked.

'We'll need to do an X-ray to find out exactly what's wrong,' Dr Fielding explained. She stepped to the control desk at the side of the viewing gallery. 'Look away, Ulf,' she said.

Ulf turned his head as Dr Fielding flicked three switches. From the corner of his eye Ulf saw a bright flash of light as the viewing window switched to X-ray mode. When he looked back, instead of seeing the sea monster's coral-covered shell, he could see right inside it. The window was displaying a black-and-white X-ray image.

Inside the sea monster, Ulf saw what looked like a huge cave.

'Sea monsters have the largest stomach of all carnivorous beasts,' Dr Fielding said.

Ulf stared in horror. Inside the beast's stomach he could see the bodies of half-eaten sharks.

'It feeds off sharks,' Dr Fielding explained. 'It injects them with venom that freezes their blood – a state known as ice sleep. The frozen sharks are unable to move, and it swallows them whole.'

On the X-ray, Ulf could see rows of gnashing teeth lining the walls of the sea monster's stomach. The sharks were being slowly devoured.

'Its digestive system appears to be normal,' Dr Fielding said. She looked up, studying the sea monster's internal organs, checking for signs of injury. She pointed her cane to a large flickering lump. 'This is its heart,' she said. 'It has six blood chambers.'

The heart was pumping frantically. 'It's in shock, Ulf.'

Dr Fielding pointed to either side of the sea monster's body where dark narrow slits were trembling. 'Its gills are hyperventilating.'

Dr Fielding stood back, looking up and down the X-ray. She frowned.

'What's the matter?' Ulf asked her.

'Up here,' she said, pointing her cane up the window to a jagged line a couple of metres above the sea monster's eyes. 'Its shell's fractured.'

Dr Fielding traced her cane around a large white organ behind the fracture. It was the size of a barrel. 'That's its brain, Ulf,' she said.

Ulf looked.

'The dark shadow in its centre is blood.'

Dr Fielding paced up and down at the base of the viewing window. 'Its brain's bleeding. This is serious, Ulf. A brain injury is life-threatening. The poor beast.'

'Can you mend it?' Ulf asked.

'I'm afraid that operating on a Redback is too dangerous, Ulf.'

Dr Fielding printed out a copy of the X-ray image then flicked a switch and the viewing window returned to normal mode.

'What do you mean?' Ulf asked.

'Watch this,' she said, reaching up and tapping the window with her cane.

Ulf saw the sea monster tilt slightly in the water. It was looking directly at them. Two rocky slabs of shell were moving apart as its mouth opened. It was the biggest mouth Ulf had ever seen.

'It's preparing to feed,' Dr Fielding said. She kept tapping her cane against the glass.

Ulf saw a snake-like limb emerging from a hole between the sea monster's eyes. It was sliding through the coral.

'That's the Redback's stinger,' Dr Fielding told him. 'That's what it uses to inject its prey with venom.'

She tapped the glass faster and the snake-like limb extended from the sea monster, reaching towards the window. 'Its stinger can sense vibrations in the water. It strikes for the heart of any creature that goes near it.'

The stinger slid towards the glass where she was tapping her cane. She was tapping the rhythm of a heartbeat. The tip of the stinger was bright blue. It opened, exposing two sharp fangs. A tongue flicked out.

'It'll try to strike,' Dr Fielding said.

Ulf watched as the stinger struck the glass with a thump. It rebounded off the window. The stinger's fangs couldn't penetrate. It struck again.

Dr Fielding stopped tapping.

'If any other beast had a brain injury, even another sea monster, I'd operate immediately,' she said. 'But not a Redback. We can't go near it, Ulf. We'd be killed.'

With the tapping stopped, the stinger coiled back into the hole between the sea monster's eyes.

'But there must be something you can do,' Ulf said. 'Orson could help. He can handle any beast.'

'Not a Redback, Ulf.'

Ulf put his hairy hands against the window, watching the injured beast. The sea monster's huge mouth slammed shut.

'Can't you tranquillize it?' he asked.

'A tranquillizer dart wouldn't get through a Redback's shell,' Dr Fielding said.

'But what will happen if you don't operate?'

'It's dying, Ulf,' she told him.

Dr Fielding placed her hand on Ulf's shoulder. '**I'm sorry**,' she said. '**We can't save every beast.**'

Ulf could see the sea monster's eyes blazing. He was sure it was watching him.

BEASTLY BUSINESS

CHAPTER FOUR

Ulf followed Dr Fielding back up the ladder, out of the viewing gallery and on to the dockside.

Dr Fielding held the X-ray printout up to the light, studying it carefully.

Ulf stood at the edge of the examination bay. He could see Captain Crab's boat moored alongside the RSPCB submersible and speedboat. The Captain was pulling his net back on board. His old face looked sunburnt and weathered from years at sea. He was wearing a thick woollen jumper and had a shiny metal hook for a hand.

The Captain looked up, picking a barnacle

from his bushy white beard. He saw Ulf watching him. 'What's up? You never seen a hook before?' he asked. The Captain bundled his net on to the back of his boat then climbed down to the dockside. He walked over and stood beside Ulf, holding his hook out. 'Sharks,' the Captain said. 'Bit it clean off.'

He polished his hook on his jumper then turned to Dr Fielding. She was still studying the X-ray. 'So, is it going to be okay?' he asked her.

'It's suffered a brain injury,' Dr Fielding explained.

'As soon as I saw it I knew something was up,' the Captain told her.

Ulf glanced down into the examination bay. Waves were splashing against the concrete wall as the sea monster writhed below in the water.

'I'm afraid we can't operate on it, Captain,' Dr Fielding said. 'It's too dangerous.'

'Too dangerous?' Captain Crab asked. 'Things certainly have changed around here since old Farraway's day.'

'Professor Farraway?' Ulf asked. 'Did you know the Professor?'

'Everyone knew old Farraway. Amazing he was,' Captain Crab said. 'He used to swim with those monsters. You'd never hear him say "too dangerous".'

Professor Farraway had been the world's first cryptozoologist, an expert on endangered beasts. Many years ago he'd lived at Farraway Hall and had founded the Royal Society for the Prevention of Cruelty to Beasts. When he died, he gave the Society everything he owned.

'I'm sorry, Captain, but times have changed,' Dr Fielding said. 'It's not safe to get in the water with a Redback.'

Captain Crab frowned. 'If you say so, Dr Fielding, but it seems awful sad to me.'

Ulf watched as the Captain took a tin flask from his back pocket. He pulled a cork from its top with his teeth then took a long swig.

Dr Fielding looked down into the examination bay where the sea monster was struggling. 'Do you know what might have injured it, Captain?' she asked.

'I just found it floating on the surface. It must have been hit by a boat.'

'Sea monsters don't come to the surface, Captain,' Ulf told him.

'Then perhaps it was an anchor,' Captain Crab said. He wiped his lips and put his flask back into his pocket. 'Well, I'll leave the investigations to you, Dr Fielding. I'd best be on my way.'

Captain Crab held his hook out for Dr Fielding to shake.

'Thank you for all that you've done,' Dr Fielding said, grasping the shiny metal.

'Fair thee well, Dr Fielding,' Captain Crab told her. As he walked back to his boat, Ulf followed.

'Did you really know Professor Farraway?' Ulf asked.

'When you're as old as me, you've known just about everyone. One of a kind, he was.'

The Captain climbed aboard.

'Would you see the Captain out, please, Orson?' Dr Fielding called along the dockside.

At the far end of the dockside the giant was throwing fish from a bucket, feeding the megamauls, beasts that looked like hairy dolphins with long tusks. Orson gave a thumbs-up then strode towards the sea gates.

Captain Crab leant down to Ulf. 'It's a bit rotten, don't you think, letting the poor thing die?' As he spoke, his eyebrows moved up and down. They were white and bushy like his beard. 'Still, I suppose it's not for me to interfere.'

'Come on, Ulf,' Dr Fielding called, heading to the Jeep. 'Orson will look after things here.'

Ulf ran after her. 'There must be something we can do,' he said. 'We can't let the sea monster die.'

'I don't want it to die, Ulf,' Dr Fielding told him. 'But it's too dangerous to go near.'

She got into the Jeep and started the engine.

'But there must be a way. The Captain said Professor Farraway used to swim with them.'

'Please, Ulf. I'm not the Professor. Things are different now.'

She pulled away. Ulf watched as she drove off along the shore of the seawater lagoon, heading round Sunset Mountain to the beast park.

BEASTLY BUSINESS

CHAPTER FIVE

Ulf rode his quad bike back into the yard and stopped outside Farraway Hall. Beside him, Dr Fielding was stepping out of her Jeep.

He switched off his engine and jumped off. 'You can't let it die,' he said.

'Listen, Ulf. I promise I'll do anything I can.'

Dr Fielding walked to the side door of the house, then turned back. 'Can you give the hellhound its medicine, please? I'll be in my office if you need me.' She closed the door, leaving Ulf in the yard.

Tiana the fairy came flying from the flower garden. 'What's up, Ulf?' she asked.

'A sea monster's come in,' he told her. 'It's been injured. Its brain's bleeding.'

Tiana gave a shiver, and sparkles fell from her wings.

'Dr Fielding says she can't mend it. It's too dangerous to get close.'

'BLUURGH!'

Ulf felt something wet land on his head. He looked up. On the rooftop, Druce the gargoyle was leaning out, dribbling.

'Druce, that's revolting,' Tiana called.

Ulf wiped the spit from his hair and watched as the gargoyle picked his nose with his yellow tongue then climbed head first down the drainpipe.

Druce leant down to Ulf, screwing up his ugly face. 'Hurted monster,' he gurgled. 'Hurted its head.'

The gargoyle dropped on to a window ledge, wrapping his head in his arms. Then he peeped out, grinning. 'Maaaarackai hurted beasts.'

Ulf watched as Druce rocked back and forth on his heels, nibbling his little finger.

'Nasty Marackai,' the gargoyle gurgled.

38

'It wasn't Marackai who hurt the sea monster, Druce,' Tiana said.

'Marackai's gone, Druce,' Ulf told him.

Druce looked down at Ulf, scrunching his nose and narrowing his eyes. 'He comes in the night with his gun and his knife. Run away Fur Face, run for your life!'

Ulf looked at Tiana. 'He *is* gone, isn't he?'

'Of course he is. Druce is just trying to scare us.'

Marackai was Professor Farraway's son. Years ago he'd lived with his father at Farraway Hall. He hated beasts. He was vicious and cruel to them so, as a punishment, Professor Farraway left nothing to Marackai in his will. When the Professor died, Marackai was sent away from Farraway Hall, but he'd sworn he'd be back.

'I bited him!' Druce said.

The gargoyle pushed his finger into his mouth then pulled it out with a popping sound.

He leapt from the window ledge flapping his stubby wings, and scurried up the drainpipe singing. 'He won't get me! He won't get me! I bited his finger and he won't get me!'

'Why don't gargoyles ever say anything nice?' Tiana said.

Ulf headed to the feed store. 'Come on, Tiana,' he called. 'Come and give me a hand.'

Inside the feed store Ulf opened a large fridge and took out a bucket of blood.

Tiana flew in after him. 'Urgh, what's that for?' she asked.

'It's for the hellhound,' Ulf told her. 'It needs its medicine.'

He looked up to a high shelf. Between a pot of **SERPENT SCOURER** and a box of **PHOENIX FIRELIGHTERS**, he saw a packet labelled **HOUND WORMER**. 'Tiana, could you pass me that packet, please?' he asked.

Tiana flew up to the shelf. With both hands she pushed the packet. It fell and Ulf caught it. He tore it open, tipping green powder into the bucket of blood. He stirred it with a stick then carried the bucket to the big beast barn, a large wooden building at the corner of the yard.

41

Ulf peered through a small crack in the barn door. Inside, in the shadows, he could see the hellhound snarling. It was a ferocious black dog with three heads. A week ago it had been brought in sick, suffering from a case of the worms. When the hellhound smelt the blood, it began barking at the door, its three mouths slobbering.

Ulf poured the blood into a plastic funnel on the side of the barn. It glugged down a length of hose and sloshed inside into a metal trough.

The hellhound began drinking, its three tongues lapping at the blood. Ulf watched through the crack in the door. He could see the fire returning to the hellhound's eyes. It seemed to be getting much better.

'It'll be out of here soon,' he said. 'Dr Fielding says it can be released when it's better.'

Tiana wrinkled her nose. 'I don't know how it can drink that stuff.'

Ulf rinsed the bucket under the yard tap. As he swirled the red water, he looked up and saw

Dr Fielding through the office window. He could see her sitting at her desk with a stack of books. She was looking through them, making notes.

'Books,' he said.

'Pardon?' Tiana asked.

'Of course! Why didn't I think of it earlier? Professor Farraway's book!'

Ulf raced round the corner of the barn, along the side of the paddock.

'Where are you going?' Tiana called.

Ulf was running to his den. He pulled open the door and scrambled to the back corner, scraping the straw with his hands and feet.

Tiana flew in through the bars on the window as Ulf prised a loose brick from the bottom of the wall. Behind it, in his secret hiding place, was a dusty black notebook. He took it out and read:

THE BOOK OF BEASTS
BY PROFESSOR J.E. FARRAWAY

The Book of Beasts was Professor Farraway's notebook from his expeditions around the world, observing beasts in the wild. It contained secrets about beasts of every kind, from trolls to griffins, from fairies to dragons.

'Professor Farraway swam with sea monsters, Tiana,' Ulf said. 'He wasn't scared to go near them.'

Ulf turned through the pages, past jottings and doodles, diagrams and photographs. He flicked past a drawing of a unicorn's heart and a note on grooming gorgons.

'There must be something in here,' he said, scanning the pages for an entry on sea monsters. He flicked past tips on growing flesh-eating plants, a drawing of a cyclops's eye and instructions on how to de-flea a biganasty. There was a remedy for demon fever, notes on the hatching temperature of phoenix ash and a step-by-step guide to unblocking the blowhole of a sandwhale.

He kept on turning the pages.

'Here!' he said. 'THE REDBACK SEA MONSTER'

It was the very last entry in the book.

The Redback is the most dangerous of all sea monsters and lives in near darkness at the bottom of the ocean. It feeds on sharks, detecting their heartbeats in the water then injecting them with its venomous stinger. In a motionless state known as ice sleep, its prey is dragged into its huge mouth then eaten alive.

At the bottom of the page was a diagram of a ball with handles on either side and a bottle connected to its base. It was labelled VENOM EXTRACTOR.

'Look at this,' Ulf said.

Tiana hovered over the page.

To handle a Redback, first remove the venom from its stinger using a venom extractor.

Hold the venom extractor in front of your heart as you swim towards the sea monster. When the stinger strikes for you, its fangs will penetrate the leather ball, injecting ice-blue venom, attempting to freeze you alive.

45

While your heart is beating, the stinger will continue to inject and its venom will collect in the flask. When the tip of the stinger turns from blue to black, its venom sacks are empty and the sea monster is safe to handle. For prolonged handling, repeat the procedure as necessary, as the Redback will replenish its venom within a couple of days.

'This is how the Professor did it, Tiana,' Ulf said. 'He knew a way to extract the sea monster's venom.'

Ulf closed the notebook. 'Come on! We have to tell Dr Fielding.'

CHAPTER SIX

Ulf raced to the house. He ran inside and burst open the door to Dr Fielding's office. 'Dr Fielding, I know how we—'

Ulf stopped.

Dr Fielding looked at him from her chair. On her desk was an old leather football with handles glued on either side. Attached to the base of the ball was an old tin flask.

Ulf stared at it.

'What's the matter, Ulf?' Dr Fielding asked.

He stepped over and picked up the dusty leather ball, holding it by its handles.

'That's Professor Farraway's venom extractor,' Dr Fielding explained. 'It was an invention of his.'

Tiana perched on the leather ball. 'Where did you find it?' she asked.

'In the Room of Curiosities,' Dr Fielding replied.

'We can mend the sea monster!' Ulf said.

'I'm afraid there's something else you need to know, Ulf,' Dr Fielding told him. She clicked her fingers, and a small hand–shaped beast emerged from a pile of newspapers on her desk, crawling on its fingertips. 'The Helping Hand dug these out for me,' Dr Fielding said. 'I think you should look at them.'

The Helping Hand spread the newspapers out and scuttled across them, pointing to the headlines.

Ulf read:

PROFESSOR FARRAWAY RESCUES A MERMAID

NO MORE DRILLING!
PROFESSOR FARRAWAY CLOSES OIL RIG
NEW MARINE RESERVE ANNOUNCED

The Helping Hand tapped its finger:
MYSTERY!

PROFESSOR FARRAWAY MISSING

The Helping Hand slid a newspaper to one side, and Ulf felt a shiver up his spine as it pointed again:

PROFESSOR FARRAWAY DIES ON EXPEDITION!

Ulf read the article below:

Professor Farraway, the founder of the RSPCB, has died on a solo expedition to examine a sea monster. The search for the Professor has been called off after fishermen discovered his boat adrift in the marine reserve. His body is yet to be found. He will be remembered for his lifelong dedication to saving endangered beasts, and the reserve is to be renamed in his memory: The Farraway Reserve.

Ulf looked up at Dr Fielding and she took the venom extractor from his hands.

'This contraption was found washed up,' she said. 'I'm afraid Professor Farraway's venom extractor doesn't work, Ulf. It would seem he died using it.'

Tiana hovered at Ulf's ear. 'That's horrible,' she whispered. 'Professor Farraway was killed by a sea monster.'

Ulf couldn't speak. He was thinking back to the viewing gallery, picturing the sea monster's huge mouth and stomach, and the rows of gnashing teeth.

'Are you okay, Ulf?' Dr Fielding asked.

Ulf felt numb. He turned and left Dr Fielding's office. As he opened the door to the yard, he heard the sound of whistling coming towards the house. It was Captain Crab.

'Ahoy!' the Captain called. He was walking past the veterinary buildings dragging a large wooden chest by his hook. Around his neck was a jam jar, hanging on a length of string. He came to the door. 'Is Dr Fielding here?'

Dr Fielding stepped out of her office and stood beside Ulf. 'Is everything all right, Captain Crab?'

'It's my boat. The blinkin' engine won't start,' the Captain explained. 'I hate to bother you but is there any chance of a room for the night? It's getting late.'

Ulf glanced across to Sunset Mountain. The orange sun was dipping behind it.

'I shan't be any bother,' Captain Crab said, dragging his chest in through the doorway. 'I'll be gone tomorrow, just as soon as I get my boat working.'

'Well, I—'

'Much obliged,' Captain Crab said.

'I expect we could find you a room,' Dr Fielding said, closing the door. She looked at Ulf and raised her eyebrows.

Captain Crab stood the chest in the corridor.

'What have you got in there, Captain?' Ulf asked. The chest was padlocked.

'This is my sea chest. I keep my possessions inside.'

Tiana flew to the jam jar hanging around the Captain's neck. 'And what's that for? It's empty,' she said, tapping it.

Captain Crab held up the jam jar and looked at the fairy through the glass. He unscrewed its lid then took a deep sniff. 'Sea air,' he said. 'There's nothing like the smell of sea air to wake up to in the morning.' He screwed the lid back on the jar and glanced up and down the corridor. 'Nice place you have here, Dr Fielding.'

He peered into her office. 'Is this where you work, then?' He stepped inside.

Dr Fielding followed him in.

'Who is that?' Tiana whispered.

'He's the man who found the sea monster,' Ulf told her.

Ulf peered round the office door, and Tiana perched on his shoulder.

Captain Crab was standing at Dr Fielding's desk. 'What on earth is this?' he asked, picking up the venom extractor and dangling it from his hook.

'That was Professor Farraway's invention for removing a sea monster's venom,' Dr Fielding explained. She took the venom extractor back. 'I'm afraid it doesn't work.'

Captain Crab scratched his beard with the point of his hook. 'Are you sure?' he asked.

'That's what got the Professor killed. He died on an expedition to examine a sea monster.'

'But I've seen him swim with those beasts,' the Captain said. 'He knew what he was doing. Are you sure that's how he died?'

'I'm afraid we can't use that contraption, Captain. I cannot risk another life.'

Ulf turned from the office door. 'Come on, Tiana,' he said, running up the back stairs.

'Where are you going?' Tiana called.

'To the library,' Ulf told her. 'To find out what really happened.'

What Ulf and Tiana knew, that no one else did, was that Professor Farraway was now a ghost. He lived upstairs in the library of Farraway Hall.

BEASTLY BUSINESS

CHAPTER SEVEN

Ulf skidded down the Gallery of Science, a wide corridor with huge framed pictures of beasts on the walls. He ran past a diagram showing the blood system of a vampire and a drawing of a dragon's eye.

Tiana sparkled at his shoulder. 'You know I don't like it up here.'

'But there's nothing to be afraid of,' Ulf told her.

At the end of the corridor, Ulf opened the door into the Room of Curiosities. Inside, artefacts from the history of the RSPCB were piled on tables and displayed in cabinets. He weaved between old veterinary tools, past a collection of antique hoof picks, a tattered canvas sail, a climbing rope from Professor Farraway's yeti expedition and the fire-suit he wore tunnelling for blaze serpents.

On the far side of the room, Ulf came to a door. This was the entrance to the old library, the room where the ghosts lived.

The door to the library creaked open.

It was dark inside and Ulf could barely see. He could just make out the dusty books lining the walls. He heard the haunted rocking chair rocking back and forth in the corner of the room.

'It's creepy,' Tiana whispered, holding tightly to Ulf's T-shirt.

A hushed whispering echoed all around and Ulf felt the hairs tingling on the back of his neck.

He trod carefully, and with each step the floorboards creaked beneath his hairy feet. He knocked into a bucket. It was full with glowing green liquid. He glanced up.

Fluorescent green ectoplasm was leaking from the ceiling.

On the upper reading level a blue mist was seeping from the wall. It formed into the shape of a girl and drifted down the spiral staircase. She disappeared through the floor.

Ulf walked between two large bookcases, glancing into the shadows. He saw a cluster of glowing orbs circling one another like tiny planets.

'Professor Farraway, are you in here?' Ulf asked. He stepped to the far wall. On a small table a candle flickered on, lighting a dusty painting of an old man in a tweed suit. He was sitting at a writing desk. His hair was grey and his eyes were smiling. Underneath, a gold nameplate read:

Lord John Everard Farraway
Professor of Cryptozoology

Ulf looked at the painting. 'Professor, how did you die?' he asked.

The table started shaking. All of a sudden the

candle rose into the air. Ulf felt a cold draught pass through him and the candle began floating across the library.

'What's he doing?' Tiana asked.

Ulf watched as the candle drifted to the spiral staircase then up to the upper reading level.

'Professor, come back!' Ulf called.

'He's being spooky,' Tiana said. She shivered, sprinkling sparkles on to the floor.

Ulf walked to the spiral staircase. He gripped the metal handrail and crept up the steps, following the floating candle. 'Professor, were you killed by a sea monster?' he asked.

The candle was now drifting along the upper reading level.

'Does the venom extractor work?'

Ulf watched as the candle flickered along the bookshelves.

'Where's he going, Ulf?' Tiana called.

Ulf followed the candle along the upper reading level. 'Come and see, Tiana,' he whispered.

The candle had stopped in front of a small black door.

Tiana flew to Ulf's shoulder. 'What's he doing?' she asked.

Suddenly, the door creaked open.

BEASTLY
BUSINESS

CHAPTER EIGHT

Ulf and Tiana followed the candle into a narrow gloomy corridor.

'Professor Farraway, where are you going?' Ulf asked.

They were on the top floor of Farraway Hall. Nobody ever went to the top floor. It hadn't been used in years.

Tiana perched on Ulf's shoulder. 'My wings are getting dusty,' she complained.

The candle floated along the corridor and Ulf followed it, pushing his way through a giant spider's web. Tiana clung tightly to Ulf's T-shirt, spitting and coughing, pulling cobwebs from her face. 'This is the last time I come upstairs with you,' she said.

The candle turned a corner. In the darkness, Ulf trod in something slimy. It squished between his toes. 'Urgh! House beast poo,' he said.

Tiana flew up, glowing brightly, her sparkles illuminating the walls. A clawhammer beetle the size of a rat was scuttling across flaking paint. A colony of sabre-toothed bats was hanging from the ceiling.

Tiana dived and hid in Ulf's trouser pocket. 'Tell me when it's over,' she said.

Ulf followed the candle, peering into shadowy rooms coming off the corridor. They were full of junk.

The candle floated around another corner. In the darkness, Ulf could barely see. He crept slowly, feeling his way along the walls. He turned the corner and saw the candle hovering outside a doorway. The candle drifted lower, lighting the door handle.

'Ulf, let's go,' Tiana whispered, darting out from his pocket.

'Wait. He's showing us something.'

Ulf turned the handle on the door. 'It's locked,' he said.

'I don't like it here,' Tiana said.

Ulf looked at the candle. 'Professor, how did you die?' he asked.

Suddenly, the candle blew out.

'Professor?'

In the darkness, Ulf felt an icy chill run through him. 'Professor, where *are* you?'

'I told you. He's trying to spook us,' Tiana said, glowing softly. 'Come on! Let's get out of here.'

Tiana flew along the corridor, lighting the way.

Just then, from round the corner, Ulf heard the sound of footsteps and something being dragged up a flight of stairs. A faint yellow light appeared, shining on the end wall. It was getting brighter. The footsteps were getting louder.

Tiana squealed and dived back into Ulf's pocket.

At the end of the corridor a figure appeared, holding a lantern. It was Captain Crab. He was dragging his sea chest by his hook.

'What's the matter with you? You look like you've seen a ghost,' the Captain said to Ulf.

'Captain Crab, what are you doing up here?' Ulf asked.

'I'm going to my room. I'm staying the night.'

Ulf watched as the Captain took a key from his pocket and dragged his wooden chest to the locked door.

Captain Crab put the key in the lock, turned it and opened the door. 'Well, don't just stand there. Give me a hand with this, will you?' he asked, pointing to his chest on the floor.

Ulf dragged the Captain's chest into the room. By the light of the lantern he could see crates and boxes, and furniture draped with sheets. The room was crammed full with junk.

The Captain placed his lantern on a table by the door and slipped the key back into his pocket.

'Where did you get that key from?' Ulf asked him.

'From Dr Fielding,' Captain Crab replied. 'This is where I'm sleeping.'

'In this room?'

'So that I can see my boat.'

Captain Crab stepped over to the window, squeezing between a large wooden crate and an old armchair. He wiped the dusty glass with his sleeve and peered out. 'There she is, safe and sound.'

Ulf stepped over and looked out. It was dark outside. In the distance he could see moonlight reflecting in the seawater lagoon and the silhouette of Orson the giant standing on the dockside, watching over the sea monster. Captain Crab's boat was in the docking area next to the examination bay.

'A Captain always sleeps with one eye on his boat,' Captain Crab told him.

Ulf looked around the beast park. On Sunset Mountain he could see the flickering lights of mothrocks, and up on the Great Grazing

Grounds he could just make out the shadowy armourpod waving its trunk in the moonlight.

'Old Farraway would've loved to have seen all this,' Captain Crab said. 'All these beasts being looked after. Such wonderful modern facilities.'

The Captain turned, his eyes glinting in the lamplight. 'He was brilliant with beasts, old Farraway. He could track a vampire in the dark. He could coax a troll from its tunnel.'

Ulf could see the Captain's eyebrows moving up and down.

'He could hypnotize demons. He could even outsmart a sphinx.' The Captain tapped his hook to the side of his head. 'Cleverhe was.'

Then he pushed past Ulf and stepped over to his wooden chest.

Tiana tugged at Ulf's pocket. 'Let's go now,' she mouthed, pointing to the door.

'Did the Professor really swim with Redbacks?' Ulf asked.

'For sure he did,' Captain Crab said. '*He* wouldn't let a sea monster die. *He'd* jump in and save it.'

The Captain opened the padlock on his wooden chest. He lifted the lid and pulled out a bundle of netting, then stood up and began unravelling it. 'Well, are you going to stand there all night?' he asked.

Ulf was staring at the net. 'What's that for?'

'It's my hammock,' the Captain said. 'It rocks me back and forth like the sea.'

'Let's get out of here,' Tiana whispered, tugging again at Ulf's pocket.

Ulf stepped over a pile of boxes, heading to the door. 'Night, Captain,' he said. He left the Captain's room and closed the door behind him.

Tiana flew out into the corridor, filling it with sparkles. 'Thank goodness,' she said. 'I thought we'd never leave.'

Ulf didn't reply. He looked left and then right. He was looking for Professor Farraway's ghost, but there was no sign of the candle anywhere. 'Why did Professor Farraway lead us to that room, Tiana?'

'It was just full of junk.'

Ulf headed round the corner and down the stairs. From the top floor, he could hear the Captain singing. 'When I was a boy my father said to me, "Yo ho ho, it's a sailor's life for thee..."'

BEASTLY
BUSINESS

CHAPTER NINE

Ulf came out of the side door of Farraway Hall
and stepped into the yard. He could see a light
on in Dr Fielding's office. He peered in the
window. She was working late, thumbing
through her books.

Tiana hovered in front of Ulf's face. 'What are
you thinking?' she asked.

Ulf was staring through the window at the
venom extractor on Dr Fielding's desk.
'Nothing,' he said.

Tiana folded her tiny arms and frowned.
'Hmmm, I know that look. You're up to
something, aren't you?'

'What if it does work?'

'You can't use that thing, Ulf. You heard what Dr Fielding said.'

'We have to try,' Ulf told her.

Tiana looked up at the sky. 'The moon's affecting your mind,' she said. 'You're talking nonsense. It's time for bed.'

The little fairy flew across the yard. 'I'll see you tomorrow,' she called. 'And don't do anything stupid.' In a burst of sparkles she whizzed over the roof of the big beast barn, heading to the Dark Forest where the fairies lived.

Ulf watched her go. He looked up. The moon was nearly full and there was only one more day until his transformation. His senses were beginning to sharpen.

He could hear the nibbling beasts scratching in their hutches and the hellhound snoring in the big beast barn. From out in the park, he heard the hoots, screeches and rustlings of the nocturnal beasts. He listened as heavy footsteps came up the track towards Farraway Hall.

'Open,' he heard.

70

The yard gate opened and Orson the giant walked in from the beast park. He was returning from the seawater lagoon where he'd been keeping watch over the sea monster all evening. The giant headed to the feed store, and Ulf went to talk to him.

'How is it?' Ulf asked.

'Not good, I'm afraid,' Orson said, turning on his bedside lamp. The feed store was where Orson slept, on a huge mound of grain. He took off his big boots, placing them by the door, then he pulled off his long socks and hung them over a beam.

Ulf sat on an upturned bucket just inside the door. 'We *can* save it,' he said to the giant. 'We can use Professor Farraway's venom extractor.'

'Redbacks are dangerous,' Orson told him. 'I'm sure Dr Fielding knows best.'

The giant reached into a barrel and took out a handful of apples. Then he sat down, leaning against the huge mound of grain. 'At least it's had a long life,' he said. Orson popped three apples into his mouth and offered one to Ulf.

'Once upon a time sea monsters never grew to be that size. The poor things were killed before they had the chance.'

'Killed?' Ulf asked. He took a bite of his apple, and chewed.

'Not any more, Ulf. It's illegal to harm a sea monster now. Professor Farraway put a stop to it. Once upon a time, though, they were killed and eaten. They were boiled up, their tentacles chopped off and their brains scooped out.'

Ulf stopped chewing. 'That's horrible,' he said.

The giant leant forwards. 'Humans,' he whispered. 'Humans very nearly killed them all.'

Ulf heard footsteps in the yard. He poked his head out of the feed store and saw a yellow light outside.

'Who's that?' Orson asked him.

It was Captain Crab carrying his lantern. The Captain stepped through the door of the feed store. 'Nice place you have here, Mr Orson,' he said.

The Captain hung his lantern on a nail on the

back of the door, and took a flask out of his pocket. 'Mind if I join you for a nightcap?'

The Captain pulled the cork from the flask with his teeth. He took a swig and smiled. 'That hits the spot,' he said.

'What have you got in there?' Orson asked.

'Captain's brew,' the Captain replied. 'There's nothing better than a drop of brew before bed.' He leant against the barrel of apples and offered the flask to Orson. 'Do you fancy some?'

The giant took the flask in his fingers and swigged a big mouthful of brew. Then he rubbed his belly. 'Tasty,' he said, handing it back.

Captain Crab shook it. The flask was empty. 'Thirsty, eh, Mr Orson? There's plenty more where that came from. Tomorrow I'll fetch you some from my boat.'

Ulf dropped his apple core into a box marked **TITBITS FOR NIBBLING BEASTS** then got up from the bucket. 'Thanks for the apple, Orson,' he said. 'I'll see you tomorrow.'

'You try to get some sleep,' Orson told him. 'You need to be strong for your transformation.'

As Ulf stepped to the door of the feed store, Captain Crab took down his lantern. 'I guess I'd better be off to bed, too,' he said. 'Goodnight, Mr Orson.'

Ulf walked round the side of the big beast barn, heading along the paddock to his den.

'Psst,' he heard.

Ulf turned. Captain Crab was following him.

'*You* could save that sea monster, you know,' the Captain whispered. His eyes glinted as his lantern swung on his hook. '*You* could use that venom extractor.' He took a step closer. '*You're* not scared, are you?'

Ulf shook his head.

'I like you, werewolf. You're just like old Farraway.'

The Captain rubbed the few coarse hairs on the side of Ulf's face. 'Sleep tight,' he said, then he turned and headed back towards Farraway Hall, whistling as he went.

Ulf watched the Captain go, then walked to his den. He lay in the straw, thinking about the sea monster.

He looked out through the bars. Farraway Hall was still and quiet. He saw Druce the gargoyle hanging from the guttering, peering into a window on the top floor of the house. The gargoyle dropped on to the window ledge as a light came on. It was Captain Crab's lantern. He was returning to his room.

The gargoyle blew a raspberry at the Captain's window then scurried up a drainpipe to the roof. In the quiet of the night Ulf could hear the gargoyle's croaky voice gurgling: 'He won't get me! He won't get me! I bited his finger and he won't get me!'

BEASTLY
BUSINESS

CHAPTER TEN

Far out at sea, a rowing boat was bobbing low in the water, weighed down by two men and a pile of bulging brown sacks. Waves were splashing over its side.

The big man Bone was rowing. 'Throw another one in,' he said.

The small man Blud was sitting in the back of the boat, shining a torch near his feet. Metal pins from hand grenades lay scattered on the floor around him. 'We've used them all up,' he said.

He shone his torch on the waves, lighting up the bodies of dead and dying fish floating in the sea. 'Look, there's something over there,' he said.

Bone rowed the boat through the fish, knocking them out of the way. He stopped beside a dead sea beast that was floating among them. It looked like a pink shark with large claws and a spiny tail.

'What is it?' Blud asked.

Bone prodded the beast with his oar. 'Dunno, but it's got a bit of meat on it. Let's stick it in the sack.' He reached over, hauling the beast out of the water, and shoved it inside a large sack from the pile.

'Now let's get out of here,' Blud said. 'Boats make me sick.'

Bone rowed quickly towards a huge old oil rig. Its high platform loomed over them on four rusty metal columns. They moored the rowing boat to one of the columns then carried the heavy sacks up a metal ladder, dragging them across the vast platform to a small black hut.

Blud knocked at the door of the hut and waited.

'Come,' a voice called from inside.

Blud opened the door. The hut was hot and steamy. Pots were bubbling on a cooker and sizzling sounds were coming from an oven.

A fat man with a thin moustache was busy chopping onions on a metal counter. He wore a white chef's apron and a tall chef's hat.

'We've got the food, Mr Ravioli,' Blud said.

'Aboutta time. Bring it here,' Franco Ravioli the chef said, pointing with his knife to a large metal counter.

Bone dragged in the heavy sacks. Spiky tails and hairy flippers were poking from their tops. They were stuffed full with dead sea beasts. He emptied one of the sacks on to the counter.

Franco Ravioli lifted up a spiny golden beast by its tail.

'*Magnifico*! A baby anglodon,' the chef said. 'I shall cut it into steaks and pan fry it with olive oil and herbs.' Blud and Bone licked their lips.

'What else did you get?' Franco Ravioli asked.

From another sack, Blud pulled out a long slimy beast with an even longer slimier trunk.

'*Splendido*! An elephant eel,' Franco Ravioli said. 'I shall stuff its trunk and grill it. Next.'

Bone pulled out a round blue beast with a huge mouth and fat lips.

'*Fantastico*! A lubbalubba. The kissing beast. I shall cut off its lips and boil them in stock.'

Bone picked out a dozen tiny sea creatures that looked like fairies. They had flippers instead of wings.

'*Marveloso*!' Franco Ravioli said. 'Water nymphs.'

He held a water nymph by its flipper and dangled it in front of him. 'I shall deep-fry them in batter. Next.'

Blud and Bone pulled out beast after beast, stacking them in a big brightly-coloured pile on the counter. Some were slimy and slipped off, and the larger ones hung over the edge, their tails and whiskers drooping to the floor.

Franco Ravioli rummaged through the dead beasts. 'Bazooka rays, serpents, diamond crabs, megamauls, skewerheads. Hmmm… I shall need more than this,' he told them.

'More?' Blud asked. 'How many more?'

'Many, many, many more. I have a Beast Feast to prepare,' the fat chef said. 'And where is the main course? Where is the sea monster?'

'The Baron is bringing it,' Blud told him.

'And what about dessert?'

'He's bringing dessert as well,' Bone added. 'He says it's a surprise.'

'A surprise? Franco Ravioli hates surprises.' He dabbed his forehead with a cloth. 'Now go and get me some more beasts.'

He waddled across the kitchen to check on his bubbling pots.

'Mr Ravioli?' Blud said, putting his hand up.

Franco Ravioli turned. 'What do you want now?'

'Have you got anything *we* can eat?'

'Get outta ma face. Franco Ravioli cooks only for paying customers.'

'But we're hungry,' Bone said.

'Hungry, eh?'

Franco Ravioli dragged the baby anglodon from the pile of dead beasts. The chef ran his knife up the anglodon's belly, slitting it open, then shoved his hand in and pulled out two half-digested sardines from its stomach.

'Here you are,' Franco Ravioli said, smiling. 'You can have these. Don't eat them all at once.'

He handed the sardines to Blud and Bone.

Blud sniffed his and wrinkled his nose.

'Now get out! *I have a Beast Feast to prepare!*'

CHAPTER ELEVEN

The next morning Ulf woke late again. He crawled from the straw and looked outside. The sun was already high in the sky, and he could see Dr Fielding's Jeep driving up the track through the beast park.

Ulf wiped the sleep from his eyes and went to meet her. 'How's the sea monster?' he asked, running into the yard.

Dr Fielding stepped out of her Jeep. She picked up a folder from the passenger seat. 'Can you come inside a second, Ulf?'

Ulf followed Dr Fielding into the house. She went to her surgery, a clean white room full of medical equipment for examining beasts. 'It's bad news, I'm afraid,' she said. From her folder, Dr Fielding took out an X-ray printout. She clipped it to a light box on the wall. 'I thought you should see this. I took it an hour ago. The bleeding has worsened.'

Ulf looked at the X-ray. The shadow on the sea monster's brain had doubled in size.

'I'm sorry, but it hasn't got long left,' Dr Fielding said.

'How long?' Ulf asked, staring at the X-ray.

'A few hours.'

Ulf pulled the X-ray from the light box. 'We *can't* let it die,' he said.

Dr Fielding put her hand on Ulf's shoulder. 'I'm sorry, Ulf. I've been up all night studying every piece of information we have on sea monsters, and there's nothing we can do.'

'Yes there is,' Ulf said.

He ran out of the surgery and across the corridor to Dr Fielding's office. The venom extractor was on her desk. Ulf grabbed it and ran into the yard. He jumped on to his quad bike and kick-started the engine.

Dr Fielding came running out of the house. 'Ulf!' she called.

Ulf wedged the venom extractor between his legs then twisted back the throttle, accelerating past the veterinary buildings. 'Open!' he shouted, speeding through the yard gate and into the beast park. He raced along the track, past the aviary and biodomes, round the foot of Troll Crag and down the edge of the marsh, the back wheels of his quad bike spinning in the mud. As he rode on to the bridge by Sunset Mountain, he glanced back. Dr Fielding was following in her Jeep, driving out after him.

Ulf twisted the throttle and accelerated round the base of the mountain, racing to the seawater lagoon. He sped on to the dockside and pulled up with a screech.

He turned off the engine and jumped off his bike, clutching the venom extractor in his hand.

As he ran to the examination bay, Ulf saw Captain Crab waving from his boat. He was holding a spanner and an oily rag. 'That's it, werewolf!' the Captain called. 'You can do it!'

Ulf stood at the edge of the examination bay and looked down into the water. He could see the huge sea monster, its tentacles coiling and thrashing.

Gripping the handles of the venom extractor, Ulf took a deep breath and jumped.

CHAPTER TWELVE

Ulf hit the cold water and his body gave a shudder. His chest tightened, his wet T-shirt and jeans clinging to his skin.

The sea monster was struggling at the front of the examination bay. It was banging its shell against the underwater gate to the lagoon. Five of its tentacles were thrashing wildly, coiling up the walls. Its other three tentacles hung limply, dragging along the concrete floor.

Ulf dived down clutching the handles of the venom extractor.

The huge sea monster turned, opening its green eyes. It let out a low, menacing bellow and its tentacles whipped down from the walls and started lashing through the water.

Ulf steadied himself, cold with dread, as the sea monster loomed large, trying to pull itself towards him. Its body was tilting to one side and its tentacles were jerking.

Suddenly, one of the tentacles lashed forwards through the water. Ulf dived beneath it and the tentacle went crashing against the side of the examination bay.

Another tentacle swept up and Ulf felt its barnacles scrape against his leg, knocking him sideways.

He heard a thudding sound and looked behind him. He could see Dr Fielding at the window of the viewing gallery. She was banging on the glass.

He turned back as another tentacle came thrashing towards him. It whacked him in the stomach, sending him somersaulting backwards through the water. He tried to steady himself, kicking his legs, and another tentacle swept over his head. He could see the sea monster moving towards him, getting closer.

Gripping the venom extractor in one hand, Ulf stared into the sea monster's green eyes. They were blazing angrily.

There was a low scraping sound and a rumble of rocks as the sea monster's mouth opened like a cave. Ulf could see the half-eaten sharks floating inside. It was preparing to feed.

His heart was thumping in his chest.

He saw the stinger emerging from its hole. The snake-like limb slid out through the coral, pulsing with ice-blue venom. It weaved towards him, sensing his heartbeat.

Ulf trembled as the stinger flicked out its tongue.

At that moment, a tentacle swung round and struck Ulf on the back, knocking the venom extractor from his hands. It rose through the water, the air in the leather ball carrying it upwards. The tentacle slid around him, its oily suckers gripping his waist.

Ulf stretched upwards, reaching for the

venom extractor, but it was floating away from him. Desperate, he kicked and struggled, clawing at the tentacle around his waist, trying to prise the suckers off. Black oil seeped out from them into the water.

He glanced at the stinger. Its blue tip was opening, its fangs ready to strike.

I'm going to die, he thought. He had to get the venom extractor.

He wriggled and squirmed, pulling at the tentacle.

As the oil leaked from its suckers, Ulf felt the tentacle's grip loosening. He kicked his legs and pushed with all his strength. Gradually he slid from the sea monster's grip, then shot upwards and pulled the venom extractor down in front of him.

The stinger struck for his heart and Ulf felt an almighty thump as the venom extractor banged against his chest, protecting him. The stinger was locked on to the ball, its fangs piercing the leather. The venom extractor was shaking.

Ulf gripped the handles tightly, struggling to

hold on. His knuckles were white and his arms ached.

The stinger thrashed, convulsing like a whip.

His heart was hammering in his chest. He could feel the ball getting colder as the stinger pumped its venom. The freezing venom was collecting inside, trickling down into the flask.

The stinger's blue tip was pulsating. Its venom sacks were emptying.

The venom extractor was working.

Ulf watched as the stinger gradually changed colour from blue to black.

Suddenly, it released the ball. The stinger swayed in front of Ulf, flicking out its tongue. Its venom sacks were empty. Ulf saw its black tip coming closer. It snaked up and down his body, probing him inquisitively. It seemed curious that he was still moving.

Ulf reached out and touched it. The stinger felt hard and scaly. It pulled back from his hand then retreated, snaking back to its hole in the sea monster's shell.

Ulf looked to the viewing gallery. Dr Fielding was calling to him from the window.

He kicked hard, swimming upwards to the surface.

A huge hand reached into the water, dragging him out. It was Orson. Ulf came up, gasping for air, and Orson lifted him on to the dockside.

Dr Fielding ran up from the viewing gallery and threw her arms around Ulf, hugging him, rubbing him to warm him up. 'Don't ever do anything like that again!'

Ulf was shivering. His teeth were chattering from the cold. 'It w-works,' Ulf gasped. 'Professor Farraway's v-v-v-venom ex-x-xtractor w-works.'

Dr Fielding took the venom extractor and ran her fingers over the fang holes in the leather ball. 'I can't believe it,' she murmured. 'It's extraordinary.' She unscrewed the flask and looked inside. It was full with ice-blue venom.

'It really did work, Dr Fielding,' Orson said.

'Professor Farraway used to swim with sea monsters,' Ulf told her. 'That's how he did it.

The Redback's stinger can't hurt you without its venom.'

'Hooray for the werewolf!' Ulf heard. He looked up. Captain Crab was standing on the deck of his boat, holding his spanner. 'I knew you'd save it!'

'We can operate now,' Ulf said to Dr Fielding. 'It's safe to go near it.'

Dr Fielding gave Ulf's shoulder a squeeze. 'You should go and get dry,' she told him.

'I'm fine,' Ulf said, standing up. 'I want to stay and help.'

Dr Fielding looked up at Orson. 'Do you think you could raise the sea monster to the surface?' she asked.

'No problem,' the giant said. He strode over to the marine store.

'Come on then, Ulf,' Dr Fielding said. 'Let's fix this sea monster's brain.'

BEASTLY
BUSINESS

CHAPTER THIRTEEN

Ulf helped Orson roll eight yellow flotation barrels across the dockside into the examination bay.

'I'll need the bungees too, Ulf,' the giant said.

Ulf went to the marine store where Dr Fielding was gathering tools for the operation. He fetched eight elastic bungee ropes and carried them out.

Orson the giant was swimming in the water, floating the barrels across the examination bay. The sea monster was below him. One of its tentacles reached up and wrapped around the giant's shoulders. 'Easy, girl,' Orson said, gently peeling the tentacle off with his huge hand.

Ulf threw the bungee ropes and the giant caught them.

Orson pushed a yellow barrel under the water, took a deep breath and dived down. He took hold of a tentacle and tied the barrel to it with a bungee rope. A moment later the barrel bobbed to the surface, lifting the tentacle with it.

Orson came up for air as another tentacle reached for him. He caught it, pulling the sea monster towards him, and attached a second barrel. The water churned, tentacles lashing as the giant pushed a third barrel down. One by one, Orson attached all eight barrels. The air in the barrels lifted the sea monster to the surface of the examination bay, and Ulf watched as its red shell rose out of the water. It looked like a coral island surrounded by a ring of barrels. Three of its tentacles lay limp on the surface of the water while the other five coiled up the concrete walls.

Dr Fielding came out of the marine store, carrying her medical bag, a circular saw and a suction pump. 'Could you bring that bucket, please,' she said to Ulf, looking back to a bucket by the door of the marine store.

Ulf fetched it. The bucket was full of wet cement. He carried it to the examination bay, following Dr Fielding.

'Could you tether the sea monster securely, please, Orson?' she asked.

Bolted into the walls of the examination bay were steel harnessing rings with ropes attached. These were used to secure large sea beasts during operations.

Orson swam around the walls of the examination bay, tying the ropes to the sea monster's tentacles, securing them to the harnessing rings so they could no longer thrash.

The ropes creaked as the tentacles pulled.

'Don't worry, girl,' Orson whispered to the beast. 'Dr Fielding will fix you up.' He stroked one of its tentacles, checking the rope was secure.

Orson pulled himself out of the water, then slid a wooden plank from the edge of the examination bay to the top of the sea monster's shell. 'She's ready for you, Dr Fielding.'

'Come on, Ulf,' Dr Fielding said. She carried her medical bag and tools along the plank then stepped on to the sea monster. She climbed down the front of its shell to a ledge a metre below. 'It's perfectly safe, Ulf,' she called.

'Just make sure you don't fall in the water,' Orson said, chuckling.

Ulf carried the bucket nervously along the plank and stepped off on to the sea monster's shell. He could feel its coral and barnacles pressing into the soles of his bare feet. He passed the bucket to Dr Fielding then clambered down to the ledge.

Dr Fielding was laying her tools out carefully. 'You might see a lot of blood,' she said.

'I'll be okay,' Ulf told her.

'Everything all right there?' Captain Crab called from his boat. 'Need a hand, do you?'

'We're fine thank you, Captain. Ulf's helping,' Dr Fielding called.

She started examining the sea monster's shell.

She ran her fingers over a jagged crack a metre long. 'This is the fracture, Ulf. Under here is its brain.'

Ulf picked out a loose piece of coral from the edge of the crack.

'Can I see that, please, Ulf?' Dr Fielding asked. Ulf handed her the piece of coral and she examined it, frowning.

'What's the matter?' Ulf asked.

Dr Fielding placed the piece of coral in her coat pocket. 'It's probably nothing. I'll check it out later.'

From her medical bag she took a pair of safety goggles and put them on.

Ulf took a pair for himself.

'Are you ready, Ulf?'

'Ready,' Ulf said.

'Then let's take a look at its brain,' Dr Fielding said. She picked up the circular saw.

Ulf stared. At the front of the saw was a large circular blade with jagged metal teeth. 'Won't that hurt it?' he asked.

'It has no feeling in its shell,' Dr Fielding said.

She turned the saw on and the metal blade started spinning. 'It's no different to you filing your claws.'

Ulf watched as Dr Fielding pressed the saw into the sea monster's shell. Bright sparks flew from the blade and it made a loud screaming sound as it cut through the coral and barnacles. She ran the saw in a wide circle around the crack.

Ulf could see a large circular slab of shell coming loose.

Dr Fielding switched the saw off. 'Right, now we need to lift it out.' She placed the saw down. With both hands she pulled at the slab of coral. 'Help me with this, Ulf,' she asked.

Ulf gripped the coral with his fingers and heaved. Slowly he and Dr Fielding lifted out the large circular slab from the sea monster's shell. It came away with a sucking sound. It was as heavy as concrete.

They laid it to one side then Ulf peered into the large hole where it had been. Inside he could see a bulging mass of spongy white flesh criss-crossed with veins.

'That's the sea monster's brain,' Dr Fielding said.

The sea monster's brain was sitting in a pool of blood.

BEASTLY
BUSINESS

CHAPTER FOURTEEN

Dr Fielding turned on the suction pump, a metal canister with a rubber hose. 'Can you get the blood out, please, Ulf?' she asked, passing him the hose. 'Make sure you suck it all up.'

Ulf poked the hose into the pool of blood around the sea monster's brain. The suction pump gurgled as blood bubbled up the hose and into the canister.

Dr Fielding put her head torch on and peered into the hole. 'We need to find the source of the bleeding,' she said. She shone her torchlight on the bulging spongy brain.

'It's big,' Ulf said.

'It needs to be. A sea monster's brain is highly specialized,' Dr Fielding told him.

She pulled on a pair of surgical gloves and pointed to two large bulges covered in a slimy membrane. 'These are the brain's cerebral lobes, Ulf. The left lobe controls the sea monster's interactive functioning: perception, recognition and communication. The right lobe controls its deep sea functioning: orientation, navigation and body temperature. I can't see any signs of damage.'

Dr Fielding felt a large bulge at the front of the brain. 'This is the visceral lobe. It controls all the internal organs.'

Ulf moved the suction hose so Dr Fielding could look for the cause of the bleeding. Then he watched as she reached down to a smaller bulge. 'This here is the occipital lobe, Ulf. It controls the sea monster's vision.' She slid her fingers down, gently lifting the fleshy tissue to reveal a thick pulsating tube. 'That's the optic nerve. It connects to the sea monster's eyes. Sea monsters can see infrared, which means they can hunt in the dark.'

Dr Fielding waited while Ulf sucked up the remaining blood surrounding the brain. He turned off the suction pump and placed it carefully to one side.

'Well done, Ulf. Now have a look at this.' Dr Fielding reached deep down the front of the brain to a small black bulge. 'This is the neco lobe. It picks up vibrations in the water.'

The neco lobe was nestled in a thick bundle of nerves. Dr Fielding parted them with her fingers and shone her torch into a cavity that ran down inside the shell.

Ulf leant in and looked down. The bundle of nerves twisted from the brain, wrapping around one another to form a single tube that was covered in scales. It ran down to a ledge behind the sea monster's eyes. 'That's its stinger!' he said. The stinger was coiled on the ledge like a snake, resting after its de-venoming.

'And it's harmless now, thanks to you, Ulf,' Dr Fielding said. 'It'll take a day or two to replenish its venom.' She reached to the back of the brain. 'This over here is the brachial lobe. It controls movement.' She carefully slid her hands down either side of the bulge. 'Oh my goodness,' she said.

'What's the matter?' Ulf asked.

'I've found the problem, Ulf.'

Gently, Dr Fielding pushed her hand in, parting the spongy flesh.

Ulf saw a huge red lump. 'What is it?' he asked.

'A blood clot, Ulf. A ball of congealed blood.' It was massive. 'The artery that goes to the brachial lobe has ruptured. The brachial lobe isn't functioning correctly. That explains why its tentacles are in spasm.'

'Can you fix it?'

'It'll be tricky. We'll have to perform an arterial bypass.'

'How do we do that?' Ulf asked.

'We'll have to redirect the blood flow with a synthetic blood vessel then remove the clot. While we operate we'll have to seal off the blood supply entirely. **It's a risky operation.** It's possible that the tentacles will be left paralysed.'

Dr Fielding took another head torch from her medical bag and Ulf put it on. 'When I say, I need you to hold that blood clot for me.'

She took out a laser pen, two metal clips and a length of thin silicone-rubber tubing. 'This is the synthetic blood vessel,' she explained, showing him the length of tubing. 'We'll use it to replace the ruptured artery.'

Dr Fielding looked across to Orson. 'We're about to close off the blood supply to the brachial lobe,' she called. 'She should go still for a while.'

The giant was wrestling with a tentacle that had slipped free from its rope. 'Right you are. Good luck,' Orson called.

Dr Fielding parted the upper lobes of the brain. Ulf could see the huge red clot. 'Lift it up,' Dr Fielding told him.

Ulf cupped his hands around the blood clot. It felt sticky and warm. As he lifted it, he saw a thick blood vessel running along its base to the brachial lobe.

'That's the ruptured artery that we have to

replace,' Dr Fielding said. She carefully clipped the metal clips to it, either side of the clot. 'Now the blood flow is sealed off, we have to work quickly.'

Ulf glanced up. All the sea monster's tentacles had gone limp.

'Concentrate, Ulf.'

He held the clot steady. Dr Fielding took her laser pen and pressed its tip to the artery.

Ulf saw a glowing red dot as the laser burned a small hole in the artery wall. Dr Fielding repeated the procedure, burning a second hole in the artery on the other side of the clot.

She switched the laser pen off and, with a micro-needle and thread, stitched the ends of the synthetic blood vessel on to the two holes.

'Now we have to cut out the clot.'

With a pair of small scissors, Dr Fielding snipped the clot from the damaged artery. Ulf felt it come free in his hands. It was heavy and wobbled as he lifted it out.

'Perfect,' Dr Fielding said. She held open a specimen bag and Ulf dropped the clot inside it. 'Now let's see if the bypass has worked.'

She unfastened the metal clips.

Ulf could see blood starting to flow through the synthetic artery. 'You've mended it!' he said.

'Don't get your hopes up, Ulf. We won't know definitely for a minute or two.' Dr Fielding looked across to Orson. 'Tell me if you see any signs of movement,' she called.

The sea monster's tentacles were hanging limply all around, attached to the ropes.

'Will do,' Orson replied.

'Ulf, could you help me get the shell back on now, please?' Dr Fielding asked.

Together, Ulf and Dr Fielding reached across and lifted the large circular slab of shell back into the hole.

'Now seal it up,' Dr Fielding said, handing Ulf a trowel. While Dr Fielding gathered her tools, Ulf grabbed the bucket of wet cement. He spread the cement into the circular cut in the shell, and then along the jagged crack.

'Orson, can you start to release the tentacles?' Dr Fielding called. The giant walked around the top of the examination bay, untying the tentacles from the metal rings. Ulf saw them fall limply in the water.

'They're not moving,' he said to Dr Fielding.

She was climbing up the sea monster's shell. She carried her tools across the wooden plank to the dockside. 'Come on, Ulf,' she called.

Ulf clambered after her carrying the bucket.

Orson pulled the plank from the top of the sea monster then all three stood watching and waiting. Orson put his hand on Ulf's shoulder. 'You've done your best,' he said.

The sea monster's tentacles still weren't moving.

The giant knelt beside Ulf and pointed to the far corner of the examination bay. 'Look,' he whispered. The tip of one of the tentacles twitched.

Then at the opposite side of the examination bay another tentacle started twitching. It slowly stirred in the water.

'It's working!' Ulf said.

One by one, all of the tentacles slowly came to life, calmly swaying back and forth in the water. They began exploring the examination bay, feeling the walls and touching the flotation barrels. The tip of one tentacle reached up and felt the mended section of shell where the operation had been performed.

'I'll leave the flotation barrels on while the cement sets,' Orson said to Dr Fielding. 'It will give her time to get her strength back.'

'Thank you, Orson,' Dr Fielding replied.

'Is the sea monster going to be all right now?' Ulf asked.

Dr Fielding smiled. 'She's going to be fine, Ulf, thanks to you.'

CHAPTER FIFTEEN

Ulf heard an engine start, and black smoke belched from Captain Crab's boat. The Captain stepped out on deck. 'Ahoy there!' he called. 'My boat's working again!'

'So is the sea monster!' Ulf replied.

Captain Crab climbed down from his boat and stepped on to the dockside beside Ulf. 'I knew you'd save it, werewolf,' he said, looking into the examination bay. The sea monster's tentacles were swishing gently in the water.

'Do you want me to tow it back to the Reserve for you, Dr Fielding?' Captain Crab asked. 'I can sling the net over it.'

Dr Fielding was packing her medical bag.

'Thank you, but we'll release it when it's had time to recover and replenish its venom. It'll find its own way home. We'll track it in the submersible and see that it gets back safely.'

She headed into the marine store and came out again holding a small black box with an aerial poking from its top.

'What's that?' Captain Crab asked.

'It's a tracking beacon,' Dr Fielding said.

At the RSPCB, beacons were used to monitor the movements of beasts released back into the wild. They sent signals to the RSPCB's computers, helping to build a database of endangered beast populations throughout the world.

Dr Fielding handed the beacon to Orson. 'Would you mind attaching it for me, please?'

'No problem,' Orson said.

Ulf watched as the giant jumped into the examination bay and swam to the sea monster. He clipped the beacon to the sea monster's shell, then flicked a switch on the little black box. Ulf saw an orange light starting to flash at the top of the beacon. Orson swam back and heaved himself out of the water. He stood dripping wet on the dockside, smiling. 'Right then, that's everything mended. I'll be off to get dry.'

'Goodbye, Mr Orson,' the Captain said. 'I should be going too. Now that my boat's working.' He held out his hook, and Orson shook it with his finger.

'Goodbye, Captain,' the giant said. Orson strode off down the dockside, his boots squelching as he went.

'You should go and get dry too, Ulf,' Dr Fielding said, feeling his damp T-shirt. It was still wet from when he'd been in the water.

Ulf looked down at the sea monster.

'Don't worry, Ulf. I'll make sure it's comfortable, and we'll do your inspection as soon as I get back.'

Every month, before the full moon, Dr Fielding gave Ulf a full physical examination, monitoring his transformation from boy to wolf.

'Goodbye then, werewolf,' Captain Crab said.

'Thanks for your help, Captain,' Ulf replied.

He walked to his quad bike and kick-started the engine.

* * *

Captain Crab watched the werewolf and the giant leave. He narrowed his eyes and turned to Dr Fielding. She was holding the venom extractor. 'I'm still amazed that this worked,' she said.

The Captain grinned. 'Good old Professor Farraway,' he said. He followed her as she walked to her Jeep and placed the venom extractor on the back seat.

'Captain, can I ask you something?' Dr Fielding said.

'Why, of course,' Captain Crab replied. 'Is something the matter?'

She took a piece of coral from her pocket. 'Did you notice anything suspicious out on the Farraway Reserve?'

'Such as?'

'Poachers,' Dr Fielding replied.

Captain Crab raised his bushy eyebrows. 'Now why would you ask that?'

She showed him the piece of coral. 'This is part of the sea monster's shell.' The coral's edge was jagged and broken, and had black flecks of gunpowder on it. 'It's as if its injury was caused by a blast.'

'What do you mean, Dr Fielding?'

'Shock fishing,' she said. 'It's a method of poaching sea beasts. Explosives are used to stun them, causing them to float to the surface. It was outlawed over fifty years ago.'

'I didn't see any poachers,' Captain Crab told her.

Dr Fielding picked up her phone from the front seat of her Jeep. She tapped a number into the keypad. 'Hello, this is Dr Fielding from the RSPCB. Could you put me through to the department for National and International Criminal Emergencies?'

'NICE?' Captain Crab asked.

'It's just a precaution, Captain,' Dr Fielding told him. 'Hello, is that the department for National and International Criminal Emergencies? I'd like you to check something. Could you send a boat out to the Farraway R——'

Captain Crab knocked the telephone from Dr Fielding's hand and kicked it into the lagoon. 'Oops,' he said.

'Captain! What are you doing?'

'I shouldn't worry about poachers,' the Captain replied. He stared at Dr Fielding. 'Now I'd like that venom extractor if I may.'

Dr Fielding glanced at the venom extractor on the back seat of the Jeep. 'What on earth for?'

Captain Crab grinned. 'Oh, Dr Fielding, I've wanted it all along. Why do you think I went to all the trouble of bringing you a sea monster? I needed its venom.'

Dr Fielding grabbed the venom extractor and held it behind her back.

'You see, I knew that the venom extractor worked,' the Captain said stepping closer.

'Stay away from me.'

'Professor Farraway wasn't killed by a sea monster. He returned from his expedition safe and sound.'

'What are you talking about?' Dr Fielding said. 'I'd like you to leave now.'

Captain Crab laughed.

Dr Fielding jumped into the Jeep clutching the venom extractor. She fumbled with her keys, trying to start the engine.

'In a hurry, are you, Dr Fielding?' Captain Crab asked. The engine started. Captain Crab slid a spanner from his sleeve and struck Dr Fielding on the head.

She slumped in her seat. He dragged her out and carried her to his boat, tying her hands and feet. Then he got into the Jeep and picked up the venom extractor. He unscrewed the flask and peered at the venom inside. He smiled.

'AND NOW TO GET DESSERT,' he said.

CHAPTER SIXTEEN

Back at Farraway Hall, Ulf and Orson were in the feed store. Ulf was sitting on a bale of hay, wrapped in a blanket, warming himself up.

Tiana the fairy flew in through the doors. 'You're wet!' she said.

'Ulf saved the sea monster,' Orson told her. The giant was hanging his wet boots up by their laces. Beside them his socks were dripping.

Tiana perched on a barrel. 'You went in the water with the sea monster, Ulf? You could have been killed!'

'The venom extractor works,' Ulf told her.

'You're crazy, Ulf.'

'He's a werewolf,' Orson said. 'He's brave.' The giant was drying his bald head with a patchwork towel stitched together from old sacks.

Ulf was rubbing the hair on his arms. He could feel it growing longer. In just a few hours the full moon would rise and he would change from boy to wolf.

His ears twitched.

He heard the sound of the Jeep's engine pulling into the yard, and looked out through the large wooden doors. Captain Crab was sitting in the driver's seat.

'I forgot my things,' the Captain called, stepping out of the Jeep.

'Where's Dr Fielding?' Ulf asked.

'She's just making the sea monster comfortable.'

Captain Crab stepped into the feed store. 'How are you feeling, Mr Orson? Nice and warm yet?'

'I'm fine, thanks,' Orson said.

From his back pocket, Captain Crab took out a tin flask. 'Fancy a drop of brew?' he asked. 'It'll warm you up.'

'Don't mind if I do, Captain. Thank you.'

Captain Crab turned to Ulf. 'Would you mind doing me a favour?' he asked. He handed Ulf a key. 'Would you fetch my sea chest for me? I left it up in my room.'

Ulf took the key.

'It won't take you long,' the Captain said. 'The fairy can go with you.'

'Me?' Tiana asked. 'But it's dusty up—'

'Come on, Tiana,' Ulf said, and he headed out into the yard.

★   ★   ★

Captain Crab watched as Ulf and Tiana went in through the side door of Farraway Hall. 'He's very helpful, that werewolf boy. And brave too.'

The Captain handed the flask to Orson. 'Here you are,' he said.

Orson held the flask in his fingers.

'It's a nice big one, isn't it?'

'It's all right, you can drink it all.'

Orson took a big swig, draining the tin flask.

'Cor, that's—' Orson's lips froze. His skin turned icy blue.

Captain Crab gave him a gentle poke with his hook and Orson toppled back as stiff as a board on to the mound of grain.

'Have an ice sleep, Mr Orson,' the Captain said, grinning. He fetched the tow-rope from the Jeep and tied it around the giant's ankles.

CHAPTER SEVENTEEN

Ulf climbed the stairs to the top floor of the house and walked along the gloomy corridor.

Tiana flew beside him. 'I don't know why he couldn't get it himself,' she said.

Ulf stopped at the door to Captain Crab's room and turned the key in the lock. He stepped inside, put the key in his pocket and started looking for the Captain's chest.

Tiana flew in after him and landed on a table with a puff of dust. She sneezed and shook her wings. 'How could he sleep in here? It's filthy,' she said.

The Captain's hammock was lying in a heap

on the floor. His lantern and jam jar were standing in the corner by the door.

Tiana looked for the Captain's chest. 'Which one is his?' she asked. The room was full of chests. There were lots of them, and boxes and crates, and furniture covered in white sheets.

'I think his sea chest was brown,' Ulf said.

'They're all brown,' Tiana replied.

Ulf stepped to a chest by the wall and lifted its heavy wooden lid.

He gasped. Inside were two trolls' heads. Their skin was green and leathery and their snouts were shrivelled.

'Uuurrgghh!' Tiana cried, flying above them.

Ulf opened another chest. Inside he saw a vampire owl. Its feathers were dusty and it was stuffed with straw. He opened another and found the tail of a mermaid, chopped off and curling at its end. He pulled the corner of a white sheet. Underneath was a dead phoenix in a glass dome. Its wings were spread and held up with wire. Then he pulled the sheet from a glass cabinet.

Tiana screamed. Inside the cabinet were row upon row of fairies, pinned flat against a black velvet board. Their wings were dry and cracked. Tiana flew to Ulf's shoulder, shaking. 'They're all dead, Ulf. This room's full of dead beasts!'

Ulf pulled open chest after chest, then box after box. He found the blubbery head of a wartolump, a pickled impossipus in a glass tank, and a stuffed gorgon with its feet nailed to a plank of wood. Its eyes stared blankly at him.

'Who could have done this?' Tiana said. 'It's so cruel!'

She covered her eyes with her hands.

Under another sheet Ulf saw a pair of brown leather shoes. He lifted the sheet up and saw two trouser legs and then a bony hand on the arm of a chair. It was holding a tea cup. Ulf whipped the sheet off and froze. 'Tiana, I think I know why Professor Farraway's ghost brought us here,' he said, trembling.

Beneath the sheet, sitting in an armchair, was a human skeleton dressed in a tweed suit.

Tiana peered between her fingers. 'Professor Farraway!'

Ulf stared at the skeleton in the chair. It was Professor Farraway's body. His bones were shiny and polished.

'But the Professor died on an expedition out at sea. He was killed by a sea monster,' Tiana said.

Just then, Ulf heard footsteps coming up the stairs.

'When I was a boy, my father said to me, "Yo ho ho, it's a sailor's life for thee".'

Captain Crab appeared at the doorway. 'Well, well, so you found him then,' he said, looking at the skeleton. The Captain glanced around the room at the open boxes and leant down, stroking one of the trolls' heads. He looked at Ulf. 'Now it's your turn to die, werewolf!'

Captain Crab picked up his hammock and threw it over Ulf. Ulf tried to claw his way out but the Captain held him down.

Ulf scratched at the Captain's face, and the

Captain's skin tore off in shreds. It was made of rubber.

Tiana hurled herself at the Captain, tugging at his eyebrows and his nose. They came off in her hands. Underneath was a face that was twisted with hatred like a rotten apple core.

'Marackai!' Ulf said, staring.

'*Baron* Marackai to you, werewolf.'

'You're not a captain at all!' Tiana said. She bit Marackai's ear.

Baron Marackai laughed. 'Didn't hurt, fairy!' He pulled his ear off, along with what was left of his rubber mask. Then he lunged at Tiana with his hook. It missed and dug into a table. The Baron pulled his arm back and his hook came off. Underneath was a hand with its little finger missing.

As Ulf struggled in the net, the Baron grabbed his jam jar, unscrewed the lid and slammed it over Tiana, trapping her inside.

Ulf kicked Baron Marackai's ankle.

'Ouch!' the Baron said. He seized hold of Ulf with both hands, carrying him struggling in the net. 'Couldn't you find my sea chest?' he asked. 'Here it is. It's the empty one. I was saving it for you!'

He kicked open the lid of a wooden chest and bundled Ulf inside.

'Help!' Ulf shouted, kicking and struggling. 'Orson! Help!'

'The giant's asleep,' Baron Marackai said. He stamped his boot on to Ulf's stomach, pinning him inside the sea chest. 'And he won't wake up in a hurry.'

The Baron laughed. 'Haha hahaa haaaahaah! I gave him a drop of sea monster venom. Just like I gave my father.' He glanced at Professor Farraway's skeleton in the chair. 'My father wasn't killed by a sea monster. He returned home from his expedition with a flask full of sea monster venom. Unfortunately for him though, he discovered my little collection here and threatened to throw me out of the house, so I slipped the venom into his tea.'

'You murdered him!'

'Not officially. Not according to the newspapers!'

Baron Marackai laughed. 'I threw his things in the sea and set his boat adrift so it looked like he'd had a little accident. I think he looks rather good among my trophies, though, don't you? You'll look good, too – when you're stuffed!'

'You'll never get away with it!' Ulf shouted. 'Dr Fielding—'

'I'm afraid she won't hear you, werewolf. She's a little tied up at the moment.'

Baron Marackai grinned. 'I'm taking back what's *mine*!' he said. 'This is *my* house and *my* land, and every beast in your precious beast park will soon be dead! THE RSPCB IS DOOMED!'

The Baron lifted his boot. 'Now, if you'll excuse me, I have a Beast Feast to attend.'

He slammed the lid of the chest shut.

Inside, everything went dark. Ulf was trapped. 'Let me out!' he shouted, pushing against the lid.

The Baron fastened the padlock on the chest. 'Help!'

Ulf heard the Baron heading out of the room.

'When I was a boy, my father said to me, "Yo, ho, urgh—" he drank his cup of tea.'

Ulf banged against the lid of the chest. He could hear the sound of the Jeep starting up and driving out through the yard. 'Help!' he called. 'Let me out!'

BEASTLY
BUSINESS

CHAPTER EIGHTEEN

It was pitch dark inside the chest.

'Help!' Ulf shouted.

He was tangled in the netting, struggling to free himself. The net cut into his skin as he shook from side to side and kicked against the lid of the chest.

'Help! Help me, Tiana!'

There was no answer. He tried to bash the lid with his fist, but the net was wrapped tightly around him. He could hardly move.

'Someone help me!' he called.

He was stuck. He lay in the dark and listened. The only sound he could hear was his own breath.

132

'Help me!' he called.

As time passed, he could feel himself getting hot and dizzy. It was airless inside the chest. He was thinking about Orson and Dr Fielding, and what awful things might be happening to them. He had to stop the Baron.

Suddenly, from out in the room he heard an almighty crash and the sound of breaking glass. Someone was clambering over the crates and furniture.

'Orson? Dr Fielding? Is that you?' Ulf called.

He heard the padlock rattling on the side of the chest. Then he heard the sound of wood splintering as the padlock broke free.

The lid flew open.

'Druce!' Ulf said. It was Druce the gargoyle!

'Drucey to the rescue!' the gargoyle gurgled. He flicked out his long yellow tongue and licked Ulf's face.

Ulf struggled to his feet and tore off the net. 'Thank you, Druce,' he said.

Druce leapt on to a table and pointed to Professor Farraway's skeleton. 'Professor?' he gurgled. He leant forwards and prodded the skeleton. 'Professor dead.'

Ulf could hear a rattling sound, and saw the jam jar rolling on the floor. Tiana was inside, beating her hands against the glass. Ulf picked the jar up and unscrewed the lid.

Tiana flew out in a burst of sparkles. Her face was pale and she was shaking. She took a deep breath then scrunched up her tiny fist. 'I hate Baron Marackai!' she said.

Ulf ran to the broken window and looked out. In the distance, he could see the Baron's boat motoring out of the seawater lagoon. The boat was dragging something behind it in the water. 'The sea monster! He's got the sea monster!'

Tiana flew out of the window and hovered high in the air. 'And Orson!' she called. 'He's got Orson too!'

Ulf could just make out the giant shape of Orson's body on the deck of the boat. 'Meet me in the yard, Tiana!'

Ulf clambered over the boxes. 'Look after this

place, Druce,' he said, taking the key from his pocket and placing it on the table beside the gargoyle. 'You're in charge now.'

Druce was stroking Professor Farraway's bony hand. 'I'm in charge, Professor. Drucey in charge.'

Ulf ran from the room, down into the yard, and Tiana flew to meet him as he sped off on his quad bike. She perched on the handlebars, clinging to the speedometer. 'Hurry, Ulf!' she said.

'Open!' Ulf called. He raced through the gate and into the beast park. The needle on the speedometer pointed to fifty miles an hour. He skidded past Troll Crag and through the marsh, heading for the lagoon. He roared along the shore to the dockside and slammed on his brakes.

'Dr Fielding,' he called, looking around. Dr Fielding's glasses lay broken on the ground.

'He's taken her too!' Tiana said.

'We've got to catch him,' Ulf replied. He jumped off his bike and ran to the RSPCB speedboat. A spanner was sticking from its dashboard and wires were hanging out. The controls had been smashed.

Ulf looked out to sea. The Baron's boat was disappearing over the horizon.

'We'll never catch him now,' Tiana said.

'Yes, we will,' Ulf told her. 'We can take the submersible.'

He ran along the dockside to the RSPCB's orange underwater-reconnaissance vehicle. It was half-submerged in the water. He untied its mooring rope and stepped on to the metal hull, then lifted up the hatch to get in.

Tiana hesitated. She'd never been underwater before. 'How can we follow them under the water? We won't be able to see them.'

'We can track the sea monster. Its beacon will show up on the submersible's computer. Come on!'

Ulf started climbing down a short ladder. Tiana flew in, and Ulf reached up and closed the hatch.

He climbed into the submersible's cockpit

and looked out through the viewing sphere, a bubble-shaped window at the front.

'Are you sure you know how to work this?' Tiana asked, flying past a row of red buttons. The inside of the submersible was dotted with switches and dials.

Ulf flicked a switch. The controls lit up and the engine hummed. He checked the power levels and tapped the pressure gauge. Then he turned on the navigation system and a blue screen appeared in a panel on the wall. It was an electronic map. In the centre of the screen was a white cross indicating the submersible's position. To the west an orange dot was flashing. It was moving away from them. 'That's the sea monster's beacon,' Ulf said.

Tiana flew to the viewing sphere. 'Full steam ahead!' she said. 'FOLLOW THAT SEA MONSTER!'

Ulf pushed the control stick forwards and the submersible's thrusters powered up.

BEASTLY
BUSINESS

CHAPTER NINETEEN

As the submersible pulled away from the dock, Ulf turned a metal wheel, emptying the pressure tanks. The submersible began to dive. A depth gauge on the control panel showed its descent: one metre, two metres, three metres, four metres, five metres...

Bubbles rose in front of the viewing sphere as the four thrusters propelled the submersible through the lagoon.

Ulf could see sea beasts in underwater enclosures. They passed a golden sea serpent with a bulge in its belly where it had swallowed an anchor, a yellow-finned sea monkey, a clump of carnivorous seaweed and a flaming squid that was glowing underwater, burning red with fire.

They headed to the sea gates. As the submersible approached, the automatic gates opened to let it through.

They sped out into the ocean, and Ulf looked through the viewing sphere. Sunlight was filtering through the water, sparkling on shoals of silvery fish.

He was in the wild. Ahead stretched mile after mile of deep blue sea.

Ulf checked the navigation system. The orange dot marking the sea monster's position was moving steadily to the west.

'Hold on tight, Tiana,' he said. Ulf set the thrusters to turbo drive and the submersible surged forwards.

Tiana hovered at the viewing sphere, pressing her hands to the glass. The submersible was speeding above the seabed.

Ulf looked down. Rocks and sand blurred beneath them. They overtook a shark, its teeth flashing as it turned.

Ahead, columns of seaweed as tall as trees rose from the ocean floor. Green and purple leaves hung in the water like ribbons. It was an underwater kelp forest.

The submersible powered forwards and long swishing kelp leaves slapped against the viewing sphere. The forest stretched as far as Ulf could see and, all around, seals were playing in the weed. The thrusters groaned as ribbons of seaweed tangled in the propellers. Ulf reduced the power and steered carefully, weaving the submersible in and out between the swaying green columns.

Gradually, the sea ahead became clearer as they pushed through the other side of the kelp forest, back into open water. The seabed was sandy.

Ulf checked the navigation system. The sea monster's beacon was still heading west.

'Where's the Baron taking it?' Tiana asked.

Ulf shrugged.

He looked through the viewing sphere as they passed a turtle burrowing for urchins. It was digging with its flippers, throwing up a cloud of sand.

'Look, Ulf,' Tiana said, pointing ahead. In front of them on the seabed was an old ship, half buried in the sand. On the ship's mast was a tattered black flag with a skull and crossbones. 'It's a pirate ship,' she said.

As they passed above it, Ulf looked down. The ship was covered in barnacles, and seaweed was hanging from its rigging, swishing in the current. He saw a rusty old cannon pointing from its side, then a huge eel wriggling from a porthole.

The submersible sped on, keeping a steady course. For over an hour, they tracked the sea monster further out to sea, passing mile after mile of sandy seabed.

In time they came to the edge of a coral reef. It stretched on for miles. As the submersible powered above it, Ulf stared at the corals and the rocks. They were all different colours: turquoise, emerald, scarlet and amber. He could see fish darting in and out of crevices and cracks. He saw starfish, jellyfish and sea anenomes.

'It's pretty here,' Tiana said. She was hovering at the viewing sphere, her tiny hands pressed to the glass.

Ulf checked the navigation system. Dotted around the orange light of the sea monster, he could see other lights of different colours.

'Look at this, Tiana,' he said. 'Beast beacons. There are beasts here.'

Tiana flew over to the screen. 'Where are we?' she asked.

They looked out through the viewing sphere and saw a silvery tail swimming up ahead. As they motored towards it, a beast turned in the water. It had the upper body and head of a woman with long silvery hair.

'It's a mermaid!' Tiana said, fluttering her wings. The mermaid swam deep down, hiding behind a bank of coral. Ulf looked to the side and saw water nymphs sparkling in the water. They were fluttering their tiny fins, swimming in circles chasing each other.

'They're just like fairies!' Tiana said.

Ulf glanced at the navigation screen. The sea monster's orange light had stopped moving. They were closing on it.

Suddenly, Tiana yelped. Ulf looked up and saw a red sea beast swimming alongside the submersible, bumping its long snout against the viewing sphere. Its jaws opened in a grin, exposing rows of razor-sharp teeth.

Ulf saw a beacon attached to its tail. 'It's a crocodon,' he said. The beast swished its barbed tail then shot off through the water. Ulf watched it disappear into the distance.

Then he stared. Ahead in the water he could make out four dark metal columns rising from the seabed.

He cut the thrusters, and the submersible slowed. 'I know where we are, Tiana. This is the Farraway Reserve.'

Ulf twisted the metal wheel, and the pressure tanks filled. The submersible started to rise.

At a couple of metres below the surface, he wound the wheel back up, bringing the submersible to a halt. He reached to the ceiling and cranked a metal handle, raising the periscope. Through the periscope Ulf could see above the water. The four metal columns were supporting a huge industrial platform with buildings on it and cranes leaning from its side.

It was the old oil rig. Moored to one of the thick metal columns was Baron Marackai's boat.

BEASTLY
BUSINESS

CHAPTER TWENTY

Ulf drove the submersible beneath the old oil rig and surfaced alongside Baron Marackai's boat. As he opened the hatch, he glanced to the horizon. The sun was low and evening was setting in. It wouldn't be long until night came, and with it the moon and Ulf's transformation.

Tiana flew out and hovered above the Baron's boat, peering into the wheelhouse. 'They're not here,' she said. She flew to the rear of the boat. 'The sea monster's gone too.'

Ulf looked up. The oil rig platform loomed over them like a large black machine. Long metal chains with hooks hung down from its edge. He clambered out of the submersible and tied its mooring rope to a metal column. Then he reached out and took hold of a rusty metal ladder. Its rungs were caked with slippery seaweed. He started climbing. 'Come on, Tiana. We have to find Orson and Dr Fielding.'

At the top of the ladder Ulf stepped on to the platform of the old oil rig. It was huge. He could see rusty sheds and old machinery: cranes, winches and fork-lift trucks. Ahead, painted in white on the ground, he saw a big letter **H** in a circle, and on the far side of the rig was a drilling tower and a large warehouse.

'It looks deserted,' Tiana said.

'Professor Farraway closed it down years ago,' Ulf told her.

Ulf heard the ***thwock thwock thwock*** of helicopter blades. He looked up. A helicopter was flying towards the oil rig. 'Hide, Tiana!' he said.

They hid behind a rusty crane as the helicopter hovered above the platform, touching down on the big letter **H**. Ulf watched as the helicopter blades slowed. Twelve humans stepped out from it on to the oil rig: six men in black suits and six women in long dresses.

'Who are they?' Tiana asked.

Across the platform, Ulf saw the door of a black hut opening. A man came out and strode towards the helicopter. 'Look! It's Baron Marackai!' he whispered.

The Baron was no longer dressed in Captain's clothes. He was wearing a long fur coat with a high fur collar, giranha-belly trousers and serpent-skin boots.

One of the men from the helicopter stepped forwards. He handed the Baron a leather briefcase and the Baron opened it. The briefcase was stuffed with bank notes.

'Money!' Tiana said.

Baron Marackai snapped the case shut. 'That'll do nicely,' he said.

The guests each shook the Baron's hand. 'Thank you... *Merci... Danke... Gracias... Arigato... Teshekurler...*'

'Come this way,' the Baron told them, leading them across the platform. 'Everything is prepared.'

'Let's follow them,' Ulf whispered.

Ulf and Tiana dashed across the helipad to the black hut. Ulf peered round its side. Baron Marackai was taking his guests to the warehouse on the far side of the rig.

Tiana tapped Ulf's shoulder. 'Look in here,' she said, peering through a steamy window into the black hut. Inside was a kitchen. A fat man wearing a white chef's hat was lifting the lid of a saucepan. He dipped his finger in a dark brown sauce then licked it. He smiled, wiped his finger on his thin moustache, then looked in the glass door of an oven.

Ulf turned and glanced back round the side of the hut. Baron Marackai was sliding open a huge metal door at the end of the warehouse. He led his guests inside.

'Come on,' Ulf said, running to follow them.

'Stop, Ulf,' Tiana called, as two men came out of the warehouse.

Ulf ducked behind a fork-lift truck. Tiana

flew beside him. They watched as the men walked across the platform towards the black hut. They were both dressed in white shirts and pink bow ties.

One was small and was dabbing his nose with a red rag. 'Blud do this. Blud do that. Pah!' he said.

The other man was big, with a thick beard. 'My shirt's too tight,' he said.

'Why do *we* have to serve the food?' the small man complained. 'Why can't we eat with the guests?'

They walked to the door of the black hut and went inside.

'Tiana, we have to find Orson and Dr Fielding,' Ulf said. They headed to the warehouse and peered through the doorway. It was enormous. Barrels were stacked around the sides, and there were piles of metal pipes, wooden crates and big rusty drills. Hooks hung on chains from the ceiling. Signs on the walls read LOADING AREA and **DANGER: HEAVY MACHINERY**.

At the far end of the warehouse, Baron Marackai was sitting at a long table. His guests were sitting either side of him, laughing and joking, pouring wine into glasses. The table was laid for dinner with a white tablecloth and silver cutlery. Candles were flickering in ornate candlesticks. There was no sign of Orson or Dr Fielding.

Tiana perched on Ulf's shoulder. 'Let's try somewhere else,' she said.

Ulf turned and saw the small man in the waiter's outfit coming out of the kitchen towards them. He was wheeling a large metal trolley. 'Quick, Tiana, hide!' Ulf said.

They dashed inside the warehouse and hid behind an old oil barrel, then watched as the small man wheeled in the trolley. It was loaded with dishes covered by domed silver lids. It rattled as the small man pushed it to the dinner table at the far end. He placed the dishes on the tablecloth in a long row.

'That'll do, Blud,' Baron Marackai said.

Blud backed away from the table, bowing.

The Baron stood up, tapping his glass with a fork. 'Ladies and gentlemen, a word if I may before we begin.' He stepped to a huge door at the far end of the warehouse. His guests turned and watched as he slid the door open.

Through the far end Ulf could see out to sea. The sun was setting and the water was glowing red.

'Look at this,' Baron Marackai announced. 'The Farraway Reserve. In these waters are treats and delicacies beyond your wildest imaginings, the rarest sea beasts known to man. For too long they have been allowed to swim freely, their delicious flesh denied us, protected by law. But I ask you, if man wasn't meant to eat beasts, why are they so damned tasty?'

Baron Marackai's twisted face twisted even more as he laughed. His guests chuckled.

'Everything you are about to eat has been caught locally,' he said. 'Which reminds me...'

He snapped his fingers. 'Tonight we have a guest of honour.'

Ulf turned and gasped as he saw the big man lumber in. He was carrying Dr Fielding over his shoulder. Her wrists and ankles were tied and her mouth was gagged. She was wriggling and struggling.

'Bring her here, Bone,' the Baron ordered. 'She can sit next to me.'

Ulf snarled.

'We've got to save her,' Tiana whispered.

Ulf crept along the side of the warehouse, keeping low behind the barrels.

Tiana flew beside him. 'Be careful,' she said.

Ulf saw the big man, Bone, push Dr Fielding into an empty chair beside the Baron.

'Ladies and gentlemen, I'd like to introduce you all to Dr Helen Fielding of the RSPCB,' Baron Marackai announced. The Baron's guests hissed and booed.

'She's going to watch us eat, while we shall watch her squirm!' The Baron laughed again and his guests laughed too.

Ulf's elbow knocked a stack of steel pipes. One clattered to the ground and suddenly the guests stopped laughing. Ulf ducked.

'What was that noise?' the Baron asked, looking to where Ulf was hiding.

Ulf crawled behind a pile of wooden crates. He watched as Blud walked over, checking the pipes. 'It's nothing, Sir,' the small man called. 'Probably just a rat.'

'Then without further ado...' Baron Marackai said. 'Let the Beast Feast begin!'

He walked to the end of the long table and lifted the silver dome from the first dish. Underneath it Ulf saw a beast that had been skinned and roasted. It had pineapple rings on its tusks.

'Roast anglodon,' Baron Marackai announced. 'Delicious!'

The guests licked their lips.

Ulf saw Dr Fielding turn her head in disgust.

Baron Marackai lifted the dome from the second platter. Underneath was a yellow trunk cut into slices with melted cheese in the middle. 'Stuffed trunk of elephant eel.'

The guests clapped.

Baron Marackai lifted the third dome. Underneath was a big blue blubbery mouth. It was sprinkled with peanuts and laid on the plate in a smile. 'Succulent boiled lubbalubba lips.'

The guests cheered.

Baron Marackai lifted the fourth dome. Underneath were fairy-like beasts fried to a crisp. 'Deep-fried sea nymphs.'

'I can't watch,' Tiana said, holding her hands over her eyes.

The Baron picked up half a lemon from the side of the plate and squeezed it over the little fried nymphs. 'Tasty!' he said.

He walked the length of the table lifting the silver domes one after the other. Under each was a dead sea beast, cooked and ready to eat. Some were covered in batter or made into pies. Others had been mashed or barbecued and covered in sauce.

'Three cheers for Baron Marackai,' the guests cheered. 'Hip, hip, hooray! Hip, hip, hooray! Hip, hip, hooray!'

The Baron sat down and grinned. 'Tuck in,' he told them.

The guests grabbed at the food with their fingers, tearing off flippers and cracking off claws. They ripped off legs and fins and popped out eyeballs, sucking them until they burst. They shoved in mouthfuls of meat, with gravy dribbling down their chins. They slurped sea-serpent soup and nibbled slices of elephant eel. They gobbled flaming squidlets, chomped impossipus sandwiches and spread sea-monkey pate on toast. They chewed the fat from the lubbalubba lips and bit off the sea nymphs' heads.

'Fill your bellies,' the Baron told them. 'There's plenty more.'

He threw a fork at the waiters. 'Blud! Bone! Go and fetch the rest!'

Tiana groaned. 'I think I'm going to be sick.'

Ulf could feel his fangs pushing through his gums. He looked to the far end of the warehouse. Outside, the sky was darkening. Soon the moon would rise.

BEASTLY
BUSINESS

CHAPTER TWENTY-ONE

Ulf turned as he heard the sound of engines coming through the entrance to the warehouse. Blud and Bone came back in driving two fork-lift trucks side by side. They were bringing in an enormous black cauldron so big that it took both trucks to lift it. The trucks' engines were groaning under the heavy load.

Ulf could see tentacles hanging over the rim of the huge cauldron.

'And now, ladies and gentlemen, the dish of the day,' Baron Marackai announced. 'The rarest delicacy known to man: the Redback, king of the sea monsters.'

'The sea monster!' Tiana said.

'It's still alive,' Ulf told her. Its tentacles were moving.

Blud and Bone drove the cauldron to the centre of the warehouse where a hook was hanging by a chain from the ceiling. They raised the cauldron's handle on to the hook then reversed out of the warehouse, leaving the cauldron hanging. The sea monster's tentacles were coiling in the air. Water was splashing out.

'Now, may I introduce our chef for the evening: Signor Franco Ravioli,' the Baron called.

The guests clapped as the fat chef waddled into the warehouse, wheeling a cage full of tall hissing gas cylinders. He positioned them beneath the cauldron then struck a match and threw it into the air. There was a roar as the gas ignited and a huge blue flame swirled beneath the cauldron.

The guests clapped then returned to stuffing their faces with cooked beasts, chomping and slobbering, their cheeks full and their lips glistening with beast juice.

As the flame warmed the cauldron, the sea monster bellowed and the warehouse shook.

'We have to save it, Tiana,' Ulf whispered.

'Look, Ulf!' Tiana said. She was shaking.

Ulf turned and saw Blud come back in driving one of the fork-lift trucks. Upright, standing on the forks of the truck, was Orson. Ulf gasped. The giant was rigid, as stiff as a board, and his skin and lips were icy blue.

'He's dead!' Tiana said.

'No, Tiana. He's frozen. It's ice sleep. Marackai's poisoned him with sea monster venom!'

'So that's why he wanted you to use the venom extractor,' Tiana whispered.

'Ladies and gentlemen, one last surprise,' Baron Marackai announced. 'For our dessert, we will be eating chilled heart – the heart of the RSPCB's very own giant.'

The guests cheered.

Baron Marackai raised his right hand in the air. 'Death to the RSPCB!' he announced.

His guests held up their right hands and

folded down their greasy little fingers. 'Death to the RSPCB!'

Franco Ravioli gave Orson a shove and the giant toppled to the floor of the warehouse with a loud thud. Orson lay on his back, rigid and still.

From the table the fat chef took a large silver bowl. He lifted his apron and pulled a carving knife from his belt. Then he knelt down beside Orson and began unbuttoning the giant's shirt.

Baron Marackai raised his glass. 'To sea monsters and other delicacies!'

The guests cheered. 'To sea monsters and other delicacies!'

CHAPTER TWENTY-TWO

Ulf watched as the fat chef prodded Orson's chest, feeling for his heart. The knife in his hand glinted. Dr Fielding was struggling to free herself from the ropes. Hanging in the centre of the warehouse, the cauldron was turning red from the heat from the flame. The sea monster was being cooked alive.

'Beast Feast, Beast Feast, *gross gordura* Beast Feast,' the guests chanted. 'Wonderful! *Ooh-la-la! Maravilloso! Wunderbar! Sugoi!*'

They were spitting bones and wiping beast fat from their chins. 'Ba-ron! Ba-ron! Ba-ron!'

Ulf leapt up. 'Stop!' he shouted. He ran across

the warehouse and kicked the knife from Franco Ravioli's hand.

'Werewolf!' the Baron hissed.

Ulf hurled himself across the table, knocking the Baron to the ground.

'Bone, get this beast off me!' the Baron ordered.

Ulf felt a pair of strong hands grip his shoulders, dragging him off the Baron. He looked behind him. Bone was lifting him into the air.

The guests had stopped eating. They were staring at Ulf.

Baron Marackai stood up, brushing his giranha-belly trousers. 'Well, well. What have we here?'

Ulf kicked Bone in the stomach.

'Ouch!' Bone said. 'You little—'

'No need for alarm, ladies and gentlemen,' the Baron said, holding up his hand. He glanced outside through the open doors. The sky was very nearly dark. He turned back to Ulf and smiled. 'You moved too soon, werewolf. Bone, cover his eyes before the moon rises. Don't let him transform!'

The big man gripped Ulf with one arm and slapped a dirty hand over his eyes so he couldn't see.

'Chef, what is the best way to cook werewolf?' Ulf heard the Baron ask.

'Urgh! Werewolf meat is dees-gusting,' Franco Ravioli replied.

'Stick him in the oven,' the Baron ordered. 'Then feed him to the sharks.'

Ulf was carried out of the warehouse. 'Let me go!' he shouted.

Bone chuckled and tightened his grip.

Ulf could feel the cool night air on his skin. He shook and struggled, trying to bite the man's hand as he was carried across the platform. If he could just see the moon, he'd transform and be strong. But the big man's hand was clamped tight over his eyes. Ulf heard the door to the kitchen open. The air was hot and smelt of cooked beasts.

'Tie him up!' Franco Ravioli said. 'Down on the floor. Away from the window.'

Ulf felt himself being taken inside and forced to the floor, his nose pushed on to a cold metal surface. When Bone took his hand away from Ulf's eyes, Ulf saw that the metal surface was a roasting tray. He twisted his head, looking for the moon, but all he could see was the glass door of a huge oven.

He felt a knee in his back as the big man bound his hands and legs with rope. Then Franco Ravioli smeared Ulf with butter and poured cooking oil over him. Ulf spluttered as the oil splashed into his eyes and mouth. Next Franco Ravioli sprinkled salt and pepper over Ulf, making him sneeze. Then he loaded the roasting tray with chopped garlic and onion.

'Put him in the oven,' Franco Ravioli ordered. 'The bottom oven.'

Bone opened the oven door then lifted the roasting tray and slid Ulf inside. He slammed the door shut.

Ulf stared out through the glass.

Franco Ravioli's face appeared. 'After ten

minutes, please turn over,' the chef said, smirking. 'You'll be nice and crispy.'

The fat chef chuckled as he turned up the heat.

Ulf struggled to free his hands and feet. The butter and oil were seeping into his clothes. He could feel the oven warming up. 'Let me out!' he shouted.

Staring out of the window of the oven, he could see the legs of Franco Ravioli and Bone walking away. 'Now for the giant,' the chef said.

Ulf heard the kitchen door close. He could smell the onions and garlic cooking around him. The melted butter started to bubble and spit. He was sweating. The roasting tray was getting hot.

He tried kicking his legs, but they were tied tightly. He twisted his neck, looking for the kitchen window, searching for the moon, but all he could see were cupboards and drawers.

Just then, a sparkle appeared at the oven door. 'Tiana!'

'Ulf, they're going to kill Orson!' Tiana cried.

'I need to see the moon,' Ulf told her. 'You have to get me out!'

Tiana pulled on the oven door. 'I can't open it!' she said. The fairy flew off and, a moment later, returned carrying a small shiny spoon. She held it up in front of the oven door.

'Not a spoon,' Ulf said. 'The moon! I need to see the moon!'

Tiana twisted the round end of the spoon. 'The moon's *in* the spoon,' she said. 'Look.'

The shiny spoon was reflecting the light from the window. In its polished metal Ulf saw the moon, full and bright.

His eyes flashed silver.

BEASTLY
BUSINESS

CHAPTER TWENTY-THREE

The hair on Ulf's hands started spreading. His nails lengthened, turning into claws. He dug them into the roasting tray, tearing the metal. A sharp pain shot down Ulf's spine. He could feel his backbone stretching and the bones in his chest cracking. His skeleton was realigning. His tail was emerging. He could feel his muscles flexing, snapping the ropes around his wrists and ankles, ripping his T-shirt and jeans. Thick dark hair was growing over his whole body. His fangs split through his gums and his tongue started dripping with saliva. His lower jaw thrust forwards as his face twisted into that of a wolf.

He burst open the oven door and leapt on to the floor. He threw his head back and howled. Tiana flew down in a flurry of sparkles.

'Hurry, Ulf!' she said. 'You've got to save Orson!'

Ulf scrambled out of the kitchen then bounded across the oil rig on all fours. He leapt into the warehouse. Franco Ravioli was standing on Orson's chest with his carving knife raised.

Ulf howled and the chef turned towards him.

'*Mamma Mia!*' Franco Ravioli said. He threw the carving knife at Ulf.

Ulf ducked and the knife whistled past his ear, sticking into a crate. Franco Ravioli threw the silver bowl at Ulf. Ulf leapt into the air and the bowl clattered against a barrel.

The chef lifted his apron. Underneath, tucked into his belt, was a meat cleaver. He ran towards Ulf, holding the cleaver above his head, shouting: '*Attaco! Attaco!*'

Ulf was too fast. He ducked, grabbed the chef and spun him round, sending him crashing against the stack of pipes. The pipes fell on Franco Ravioli's head, knocking him out.

Ulf turned and snarled at the guests.

The guests screamed.

'Finish him, Bone!' Baron Marackai called.

The big man picked up a metal chain and swung it around his head. 'Want some of this?' he said to Ulf.

'Up here, Ulf!' Tiana called. Ulf looked up. The fairy was hovering above the cauldron. 'Quick! The water's bubbling!' she said.

Ulf could smell the sea monster cooking. He growled at Bone, then leapt, springing high into the air, hooking his claws on to the rim of the cauldron. As he grabbed the cauldron, it swung on the hook.

The guests ran from their chairs.

'Sit down, ladies and gentlemen. Enjoy the entertainment,' Baron Marackai said. He turned to Bone. 'Get that werewolf!' the Baron ordered.

Ulf was swinging the cauldron back and forth trying to tip it. The hot water was sloshing and splashing. The sea monster's tentacles were reaching up, twisting and curling.

Bone smashed the chain across Ulf's leg. Ulf howled as one of his paws slipped from the cauldron.

The water was starting to boil. One by one, the sea monster's tentacles went limp over the rim. Its black suckers were dripping oil.

'Ulf! Watch out!' Tiana called.

Bone swung the chain and it smashed against Ulf's back. Ulf howled, clinging on by a claw. He kicked his legs, swinging the cauldron high into the air. Then he pulled as hard as he could. The cauldron tilted on the hook and turned upside down.

The sea monster slid from the cauldron, crashing down in a torrent of hot water, sending the gas cylinders flying across the warehouse.

Ulf tumbled to the floor. As he scrambled to his feet, Bone swung the chain at him. Ulf grabbed hold of it and pulled, sending the big man flying into an iron girder.

'Get up, Bone!' Baron Marackai ordered.

Bone lay on the floor, rubbing his head.

The sea monster's tentacles began moving. They started whipping around the warehouse, thumping into barrels and gas cylinders, and smashing crates against the walls.

The guests screamed and scattered, trying to escape. They slipped and slid on the floor. It was flooded with hot water.

'Help! *Sacré bleu*! *Tasukette*! *Ayuda*! *Ach nein, monster*!'

Dr Fielding was tied to her chair. She was rocking from side to side, shuffling to the wall.

'Bone! Get that werewolf!' the Baron shouted. 'You too, Blud!'

Blud and Bone ran for the doors.

'Come back, cowards!' Baron Marackai called.

Franco Ravioli got up from the floor, rubbing his head. He ran out of the warehouse. 'I never cook for you again!'

From his coat pocket, the Baron took out a pistol and loaded it with a shiny bullet. 'You're giving me indigestion, werewolf,' he said.

He cocked the trigger, pointing the pistol at Ulf. 'Prepare to die!'

But as the Baron fired, a tentacle whipped in front of Ulf and the bullet ricocheted off its barnacles.

The sea monster was pulling itself along the floor by its suckers. It was sliding towards the Baron. It crashed a tentacle down on to the table, smashing it to pieces. Wood, glass, plates and cutlery flew in all directions.

Baron Marackai quickly loaded more bullets into his pistol and started shooting at the sea monster. 'Get it away from me!' he shouted.

The bullets bounced off the sea monster's shell. It wrapped a tentacle around the Baron's waist.

'Noooo!' the Baron cried, bashing the tentacle with his empty gun. He threw the gun down and started pulling at the suckers. The sea monster was dragging itself to the open end of the warehouse heading for the sea. The tentacle lifted him into the air.

'Put me dow—'The Baron's head banged on

a sign saying **LOADING AREA – DANGER OF FALLING!** The tentacle gripping him reached out through the open doors, dangling the Baron high above the sea.

With a loud bellow the sea monster dragged itself out of the warehouse and over the edge of the oil rig, taking Baron Marackai with it.

Ulf looked down. By the light of the full moon, he could see Baron Marackai falling, held in the grip of the sea monster.

'I'll be baaaaaaaaaack!' the Baron screamed.

There was a loud splash as the sea monster and the Baron disappeared beneath the waves.

Ulf licked his fangs and growled.

Tiana hovered beside him. 'Good riddance,' she said, looking down into the water.

Just out from the oil rig, Ulf saw Blud, Bone and the fat chef motoring away in Baron Marackai's boat. In the sky above, he could hear the helicopter flying off with the guests.

He ran to Dr Fielding and bit through her ropes.

She tore the gag from her mouth, and hugged him. 'You saved us, Ulf,' she said.

Ulf scrambled to Orson. The giant was lying on his back on the floor in a pool of hot water. He was no longer blue. He was defrosting.

'Wake up, Orson,' Tiana said. She was fluttering around his head, showering him with sparkles.

Dr Fielding put her hand on Orson's wrist, checking his pulse. 'He's alive!' she said.

The hot water from the cauldron had raised his body temperature. He was waking up from the ice sleep. Ulf gave Orson's face a lick. The giant's eyes opened and he shook his head.

'Are you okay?' Tiana asked him.

'That Captain makes a strong brew,' the giant said. Then he looked around. 'Where are we?'

Dr Fielding and Tiana both smiled, and Ulf's lip curled, showing his fangs.

At that moment, the sound of a human voice came from the sea below. 'Is everything all right up there?'

Ulf padded to the open door and saw an

orange boat on the water below. A man was shining a spotlight up at the oil rig. 'What's going on up there?' he called. It was an inspector from NICE.

Dr Fielding stepped to the edge and looked down. 'Dr Fielding here,' she called. 'Everything's over now.'

'Who's that you've got with you, Dr Fielding?' the inspector called, shining his spotlight on to Ulf.

Ulf threw his head back and howled at the moon.

BEASTLY BUSINESS

CHAPTER TWENTY-FOUR

The next morning, when Ulf woke up in the straw in his den, he licked his teeth, feeling where his fangs had been. His body had returned to that of a boy. He looked out at the sky. The sun was shining. It would be a whole month until his next transformation.

Outside his door, a pair of jeans and a T-shirt were folded, ready for him to put on. He got dressed then washed his face in a bucket of water and headed up the track to Farraway Hall.

Tiana came flying to meet him, weaving along the paddock fence. 'Morning, Ulf,' she said.

'Morning, Tiana.'

'You were brave last night,' she told him.

'Was I?' Ulf asked.

'Don't you remember? You saved Orson and Dr Fielding, *and* the sea monster.'

Ulf smiled. 'Where is Dr Fielding?' he asked.

'She's with Orson in the flower garden. We're all waiting for you.'

Tiana flew off and Ulf followed her to the garden at the back of Farraway Hall. Dr Fielding was holding a wreath of flowers. Orson was leaning on a shovel next to a pile of earth. His hair was combed and he was wearing his best shirt.

'Good morning, Ulf,' they both said.

In the flower garden, Ulf saw a deep rectangular hole dug in the ground.

'It's a grave,' Tiana whispered. 'It's for Professor Farraway.'

'Druce showed us the room,' Dr Fielding said, putting her arm around Ulf's shoulder. 'Baron Marackai must have brought that key with him. I didn't give it to him. That room has been locked for years.'

Orson picked up a long canvas bundle that lay beside the grave.

'The Professor's bones,' Tiana whispered.

Dr Fielding had wrapped Professor Farraway's skeleton in a ship's sail from the Room of Curiosities. 'He deserves a proper funeral,' she said.

Ulf, Dr Fielding and Tiana watched as Orson gently laid the wrapped bones into the hole in the ground. Then he took his shovel and covered them with earth.

'The Professor was murdered,' Ulf said. 'He came home from his expedition with a flask of sea-monster venom.'

Ulf looked into the grave. 'He discovered Marackai's beast collection and told Marackai to leave. Marackai used the venom to poison him.'

Orson looked at Ulf. 'Thank you for saving my life, Ulf,' he said.

'Marackai probably thought that if he killed his father then this place would be his,' Dr Fielding said. 'He can't have known the

182

Professor would leave him nothing in his will.'

'He wanted to take it from us,' Ulf said.

'And he would have succeeded if it hadn't been for you, Ulf.'

Dr Fielding held Ulf's hand as they stood at the graveside and said farewell to Professor Farraway.

'Bye bye, Professor,' a voice gurgled.

Ulf looked back at the house and saw Druce the gargoyle leering down from the edge of the rooftop. Druce bowed his head then turned to stone.

Orson picked up a large slab of rock, one that he'd fetched from Troll Crag. He stood it upright at one end of the grave. On it he'd carved the words:

PROFESSOR FARRAWAY
R I P

Dr Fielding bent down, placing her wreath of flowers on the grave. 'You would have been proud of Ulf, Professor,' she whispered.

Tiana flew down and laid a petal beside it.

Ulf traced the letters on the gravestone with his finger. 'What does RIP mean?' he asked.

'Rest In Peace,' Tiana told him.

'He'll like it in the flower garden,' Orson said. 'And he'll make good fertiliser, too.' The giant flattened the earth with the back of his shovel then walked away from the grave.

'Come on, Ulf,' Dr Fielding said, putting her hand on his shoulder.

Ulf stood up then looked to the window of the library. 'I just need to do something,' he said.

He walked to the house and went inside, heading up the stairs and along the Gallery of Science. He weaved through the Room of Curiosities to the door of the library. He stepped inside.

Ulf could hear the haunted rocking chair rocking back and forth in the corner. He crept to the far wall and stood in front of the painting. In the gloom he could still make out the Professor's friendly eyes.

'You can rest in peace now, Professor. We know what happened.'

Just then, the candle flickered on.

'Professor?'

The candle was lighting up the painting.

'It's over, Professor,' Ulf said. 'Marackai's gone.'

The candle flickered.

In front of it, on the table, an invisible finger was writing in the dust:

HE'LL NEVER GIVE UP

THE END ... FOR NOW

**Turn the page for the
exciting first chapter of
*Bang Goes
a Troll***

CHAPTER ONE

High on a snowy mountaintop, a blizzard was howling. A tall man in a long fur coat staggered knee-deep through the snow, glancing into the mouths of caves. He gripped his high fur collar, shielding his face from the wind, and peered down into a hole in the ground. 'This is the one,' he muttered. 'Blud! Bone! Over here!'

'Coming, Baron Marackai.'

Two men were trudging towards him through the snow. One was small and was clutching a rifle. The other was big with a frosted beard and was dragging a long black hose.

'Stick the hose down here, Bone,' Baron Marackai ordered.

The big man Bone poked the end of the hose into the hole in the ground. He twisted a nozzle and thick black oil started pouring out into the mountain.

The three men waited silently as oil glugged from the hose. Snowflakes were swirling around them, whitening their hair and clothes.

'It's fr-fr-freezing up here,' the small man muttered. The rifle in his hands was rattling and a snotty icicle hung from his nose. He glanced down the mountainside, his eyes following the hose to an oil tanker and a cattle truck parked on an icy track. 'Can I w-w-wait in the tr-truck, Sir?'

'Stay where you are, Blud, you snivelling runt,' Baron Marackai ordered.

'Yes, B-Baron M-Marackai. Sorry B-Baron M-Marackai,' the small man muttered.

The Baron turned to Bone and stamped his serpent-skin boot. 'Hurry up!' he yelled.

Bone looked down into the hole. 'Nearly finished, Sir.' The hose gurgled and he shook black oily drips from its end.

'Is that the whole tanker full?'

'It's all in there, Sir.'

'Splendid,' the Baron said. 'Blud, pass me the matches. It's time to smoke out the trolls.'

Blud fumbled in his jacket pocket and handed Baron Marackai a crumpled box of matches.

Baron Marackai struck a match and its flame fizzed, then went out. He tried to strike another but it snapped in two. 'These are old matches, Blud!'

'I found them on the reception desk at the hotel,' Blud told him.

'You useless fool,' Baron Marackai muttered. He took the remaining matches from the box and struck them all at once. They sputtered into flame and he dropped them down the hole. There was a whooshing sound as the oil caught fire and flames roared underground. All across the snowy mountain, thick black smoke began billowing from holes and caves.

'Get ready!' Baron Marackai ordered. He hid behind Bone, using the big man as a human shield. Blud crouched beside him.

'Not you, Blud,' Baron Marackai said. 'You're the shooter!' He pushed the small man into the open.

Blud stood shivering in the wind and snow, his eyes darting from left to right as he pointed his rifle from one smoking cave to another.

From inside the mountain came the sounds of underground beasts: growls and squeals, bellows and squawks. Beasts came hurrying from caves, trying to escape the smoke. An ice-bear bounded out into the snow, roaring. A vampire owl flew screeching into the air. A giant wraith spider scurried out, hissing.

'It's the trolls I want!' the Baron shouted.

'There's one!' Bone called.

From a smoking cave, a huge green troll charged out on all fours, swiping the air with its long tusks. It roared, snorting smoke from its nostrils. The troll saw Blud and stood tall, beating its chest. 'Oof! Oof! Oof!'

'Help!' Blud cried.

Baron Marackai peered out from behind Bone, pointing. 'Shoot it, you moron!'

Blud aimed his rifle at the troll. His teeth rattled as he squeezed the trigger and fired. A feathered tranquillizer dart shot out and struck the troll on the chest.

The troll stumbled, then toppled to the ground with a thud. It lay in the snow, face down, unconscious.

Blud spun round as another big green troll ran from the mouth of a cave.

'Aim between its eyes!' the Baron shouted.

Blud fired another tranquillizer dart, hitting the troll on the arm. It tumbled into the snow. Another troll burst out and Blud fired again. The feathered dart hit the troll on the nose.

'Behind you!' Bone called.

Two more trolls charged out from the smoke-filled mountain and Blud fired twice. The trolls fell, one on top of the other.

Troll after troll burst from the caves. There was oofing and roaring, and the whizz and crack of tranquillizer darts firing from the rifle. One by one they toppled into the snow.

Slowly, the mountain fell silent and the

smoke began to clear. More than twenty trolls lay tranquillized and unconscious on the ground.

'Splendid!' Baron Marackai said, stepping out from behind Bone.

He walked through the snow to one of the trolls and kicked it with his serpent-skin boot. 'Sleeping like a baby,' he said. 'Bone, pick out five young ones and load them on to the cattle truck.'

Bone trudged over to inspect the tranquillized trolls. 'How do I tell which are the young ones, Sir? They all look big and ugly.'

'The young ones have the softest skin,' Baron Marackai told him.

Bone knelt down and pinched a troll's cheek, tugging its thick rubbery skin.

Blud skittered over to the Baron. 'What are we going to do with them, Sir?' he asked.

The Baron rubbed his hands together. 'We shall use them in the Predatron,' he said.

'The Predatron!' Blud said excitedly.

'These stupid beasts won't stand a chance.'

'But what if we get caught, Sir?' Blud asked. The small man glanced shiftily from side to side. 'What if you-know-who find out?'

'I have prepared for that,' Baron Marackai said, grinning.

The Baron stroked the small stump of flesh on his right hand where his little finger was missing. He held his hand up. 'Now, repeat after me. Death to the RSPCB!'

Blud and Bone turned down their little fingers then held up their right hands. 'Death to the RSCPC!' they said.

'The RSPCB, you numbskulls!'

The Baron picked up two handfuls of snow and pushed them in the men's faces. 'Now load those trolls on the truck! I have important business to attend to.'

Blud and Bone wiped the snow from their eyes and watched curiously as the Baron strode off across the mountain. He was peering into the caves.

'Where are you?' the Baron called. 'Come to Marackai.'

He glanced over at a small hole about twenty metres away. The head of a creature with pointy ears and large white eyes was poking from it.

The Baron waved. 'Coo-ee!'

The creature ducked as Baron Marackai ran towards it.

The Baron reached into the hole and pulled the creature out by its neck. 'Well, well, what have we here?' he said, screwing up his nose.

It was a little grey goblin. It was dirty and wrinkly and wriggled in the Baron's grasp. In its bony hand the goblin was clutching a small black bat.

'Don't hurt me,' the goblin pleaded, its fat snout twitching.

The Baron smiled, his face twisting like a rotten apple core. 'Spying are you, goblin?'

The goblin's white eyes blinked. 'Help!' it called.

'There's no one to help you here, you revolting little creature,' the Baron said. 'The RSPCB is miles away!'

The goblin looked down at its bat. 'What to do, little bat? What to do?' he muttered.

'Give that to me, goblin,' Baron Marackai ordered.

'No! Not my bat!'

The Baron reached for the bat in the goblin's hands. 'I SAID, GIVE IT TO ME!'

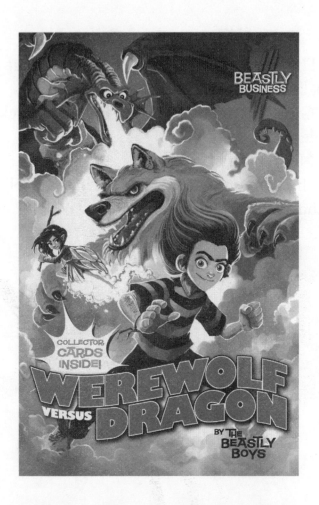

Can Ulf defeat the beast hunter?

The first thrilling adventure in the Beastly Business series.

SIMON AND SCHUSTER
A CBS Company

BEASTLY
BUSINESS

BEASTLY BUSINESS

BEASTLY BUSINESS

The Beastly Boys are **David Sinden, Matthew Morgan** and **Guy Macdonald**. They met at school in Kent, and have been friends ever since.

SIMON AND SCHUSTER
A CBS Company